# RENEGADE

## THE CAPTIVE SERIES, BOOK 2

## ERICA STEVENS

## ALSO FROM THE AUTHOR

**Books written under the pen name**
**Erica Stevens**

**The Captive Series**

Captured (Book 1)

Renegade (Book 2)

Refugee (Book 3)

Salvation (Book 4)

Redemption (Book 5)

Broken (The Captive Series Prequel)

Vengeance (Book 6)

Unbound (Book 7)

**The Fire & Ice Series**

Frost Burn (Book 1)

Arctic Fire (Book 2)

Scorched Ice (Book 3)

**The Kindred Series**

Kindred (Book 1)

Ashes (Book 2)

Kindled (Book 3)

Inferno (Book 4)

Phoenix Rising (Book 5)

**The Ravening Series**

Ravenous (Book 1)

Taken Over (Book 2)

Reclamation (Book 3)

**The Survivor Chronicles**

Book 1: The Upheaval

Book 2: The Divide

Book 3: The Forsaken

Book 4: The Risen

**Books written under the pen name
Brenda K. Davies**

**The Alliance Series**

Eternally Bound (Book 1)

**Hell on Earth Series**

Hell on Earth (Book 1)

*Coming August 2017*

**The Road to Hell Series**

Good Intentions (Book 1)

Carved (Book 2)

The Road (Book 3)

Into Hell (Book 4)

**The Vampire Awakenings Series**

Awakened (Book 1)

Destined (Book 2)

Untamed (Book 3)

Enraptured (Book 4)

Undone (Book 5)

Fractured (Book 6)

**<u>Historical Romance</u>**

A Stolen Heart

*Special thanks to my husband, best friend, and biggest supporter. My parents, for teaching me to never give up.*
*To my siblings, nieces and nephews who make life more interesting and fun. To my friends for all the laughter and character ideas, and Leslie Mitchell from G2 Freelance editing for all her hard work and encouragement.*

# CHAPTER ONE

ARIA DIDN'T HAVE to look up to know that Max had arrived. He'd been joining her here, at the same time, everyday for the last month. Even if she hadn't been expecting him, she would have detected his presence by his subtle smell and quiet step. He settled onto the ground beside her, remaining silent as he picked up a rock and leisurely skipped it across the lake. Aria handed him the fishing pole beside her, the hook was already baited and ready for him. He took it from her, casting it easily into the center of the lake.

Aria swung her feet back and forth, her toes skimming across the water. The cool water felt wonderful against her overheated skin. Using the back of her arm, she wiped away the sweat already beading along her forehead. They sat for awhile together, wordlessly reeling in the fish they caught. They kept the ones that were good to eat, and tossed back the ones that were too small.

Aria had started retreating to this spot soon after her escape from being a blood slave, and her subsequent return home. Max had found her here two days later. They rarely spoke, they didn't have to. They had both been inside that place, both been owned and used, and both of them had been forever marred by the vampires that had possessed them. The *monsters* that had owned them. Though, decidedly, Max's experience had been far worse than hers.

She had been owned, led around by a leash, and used, but the extent of her use was her own fault. She'd willingly given the prince her blood, mistakenly thinking that she was falling in love with the deceptive bastard, but that had been before she'd learned that he was engaged. Though she hated the prince now, she couldn't deny the sharp stab of sorrow that pierced her at the thought of him marrying another woman. It brought tears to her eyes every time it crossed her mind, which was far more often than she cared to admit.

But, no matter how badly she'd been hurt, no matter how much she'd been betrayed, her experience hadn't been anywhere near as awful as Max's. Though they didn't talk about it, she knew what happened to blood slaves. They were used, abused, and discarded when their owners grew tired of them. Even though Max always wore long sleeves, every once in awhile his shirt would ride up and she would catch a glimpse of the marks and burns that scarred his fair skin. She'd seen the haunted look that filled his bright blue eyes when he didn't think anyone was looking.

She'd suffered abuse while within the palace, but it had been at the hands of a human servant, and not the vampire prince. The prince had broken her heart, but he had never intentionally inflicted any bodily harm on her that she hadn't asked for. In fact, he had been unfailingly tender with her.

Though she hated to acknowledge it, she knew that if the prince hadn't taken so much of her blood on her last night in the palace, which left her incoherent, she would have given him far more than just her blood. She would have freely given him her body, and her last piece of self respect. It was a fact that she hated herself for, and tried not to think about. Especially since the thought still left her oddly shaken and aching with a need that had been left unfulfilled, and always would be.

The prince may not have been physically abusive to her, but Max's owner had been just as cruel and brutal as they'd always heard vampires were to their slaves. Aria's neck was only marred by one bite mark, one that she had yearned for so badly that her whole being had begged for it. A bite that had nearly stripped her soul from her, and left her a far different person than the one she'd been before he'd fed from her. A mark that was fading faster than she wanted it to, yet nowhere near as fast as she wished it would. She didn't like losing the mark, it was her last connection to the prince, and no matter how much she hated him, she couldn't deny that he would always own a piece of her heart. But it could only be a small piece as he had succeeded in shattering the rest of it.

She hoped that once the mark was gone she would be able to forget about the prince. Maybe once it was gone, she could move on with her life and not hurt so much all the time. Maybe she wouldn't ache constantly, the dreams would stop haunting her, and she could stop just existing and actually start living again. She would like to take pleasure in the woods again, but since her return she'd found little joy in the wilderness she'd once loved so dearly.

Max reeled his line in, deftly unhooked a decent sized bass, and added it to their growing catch. Aria pulled her dark pants up, baring her legs to her knees. She squirmed her way closer to the edge of the lake, and dipped her legs up to her shins in the water. She would like to go swimming soon, wash her hair, and clean herself. One of the few things she missed about the palace, besides the prince, was the blessedly hot showers and baths she'd taken. Diving in the lake wasn't the same cleansing experience, though she did it far more often now than she had before she was captured. Being clean every day while in the palace had left her with the same desire now that she was home.

After about an hour, Max finally spoke. "You had another bad dream last night."

Aria sat silently, she didn't know how to tell him she didn't have nightmares like he did. She didn't relive violent beatings and torture. Her dreams were about the last night she'd had with the prince, the awe she'd felt, the joy and love that had suffused her. His feeding from her had been so breathtaking, and amazing, that she still missed the connection. Something she would never admit to. It had been painful for Max when his owner drank from him, but for her, it had been a moment of pure ecstasy that had touched her profoundly. It was the loss of that joy, the loss of *him* that caused her to cry and moan and awaken at night. For her the night was not about reliving torment, like it was with Max. It was about reliving heartache.

She had never deluded herself into thinking that anything between her and the prince could last. She would have had to die eventually, the rest of the royal family, his *wife*, would have seen to that. She *had* deluded herself into thinking that he might actually care for her also. But that was before she'd learned that he was already engaged to someone else. The thought still left her feeling furious and betrayed.

Max wrapped his hands lightly around hers, trying to steady them as they shook on the pole. "The fish will know you're here."

She managed to return his feeble smile as she labored to breathe, struggled to regain control of her bruised pride and broken heart. "I don't think my nightmares are as bad as yours," she said quietly.

He squeezed her hand soothingly before reluctantly releasing her. They had never spoken about their experiences, though it was obvious that they'd both been changed forever. But Aria had gained weight while in captivity, Max had grown even thinner, his bones were still sharp against his pale skin. He had far more bruises, scars, and bite marks than she did, though her scars were mainly inside. His experience had been far more physically taxing but just as mentally abusive, and toxic, as hers had been.

"That's a good thing," he murmured.

She tilted her head, offering him a small half smile. His clear blue eyes were tender. His sandy blond hair hung about his handsome face and stark features. It was her fault that Max had even been in that awful situation. He had allowed himself to be captured after she was taken, with the hope that he would be able to get them both free. Unfortunately, he hadn't anticipated just how much of a lockdown blood slaves were placed in. Though, she'd been afforded far more freedom than he had.

She glanced down at her wrist, the one that had been scarred by the leash she had tried to rip from her. All she'd gotten for her efforts was a bloody wrist, bloody fingers, and a pissed off prince who had been so unbelievably tender afterwards.

She forcefully shut the thought down. Recalling the prince as tender and loving only reopened the raw and jagged lesions still festering upon her heart. "You never should have been there Max, I'm sorry."

It was the first time she had apologized to him for her role in his capture; she hadn't been able to get the words out before. She'd tried to apologize many, *many* times, but neither of them liked to be reminded of their time there. They both kept it to themselves in a bogus attempt to deny that it had even happened, and they were both failing miserably at it. No matter how much they sought to pretend that their captivity hadn't happened, they couldn't succeed at it.

He was silent for a moment, his gaze distant as he stared across the lake. He turned toward her, his eyes haunted, but there was something else in them too, something more.

There had only been one other man that had ever looked at her like that, and in the end he had left her shattered and broken. She was barely able to breathe through the grief that continuously clawed at her insides. The prince had ruined her, and Max didn't fully understand that yet. She hoped that one day he would. The last thing she wanted was to have Max saddened because of her again, but with the way he was looking at her, she felt it was inevitable.

"I made the choice to go after you Aria, it was my fault that I was caught, not yours. Even knowing what I do now, I wouldn't change anything. I would never leave you alone Aria, never."

She searched his face as she stared back at him. She had always found him handsome, and she still did, but it was not the dark, dangerous ruggedness that the prince possessed. Max was blond, with clear blue eyes, and an open sweet face that made many girls swoon. At one time he had even made *her* swoon. So much so that Max had been her first and only kiss, before she had met the prince. And then she had known that no matter what feelings she had once possessed for Max, they'd been nothing compared to what she felt for the prince.

And now the prince was gone, lost to her forever. Max was looking at her with the same amount of longing she'd seen in the eyes of the prince. She swallowed the lump in her throat, fighting against the tears that threatened to fall. Unlike the prince though, Max would never leave her alone, he would never betray her or use her like the prince had. Max would love her and never seek to destroy her. He would do everything in his power to keep her safe, to build her up again, and would sacrifice himself over and over for her. Even if the prince could have located her, he never would have come for her. He had a fiancée he had to take care of now, a vampire to build a life with, to have children with. She was nothing but a pitiful human toy to him.

Even knowing all of these things, why did she still love the bastard? Why on earth couldn't she love someone as caring and sweet as Max? Oddly enough, she did love Max. She loved him with a fierce sort of protective love, but she wasn't *in* love with Max and knew in her heart she never would be.

Aria shook her head, trying to deny his words. "Max..."

"It's ok Aria, one day you'll forget him, you'll move on."

"You know about him?" she whispered, unexpected shame flooded her body.

She felt like a traitor and a fool. Her father was the leader of the rebels; her brothers and Max were some of his strongest fighters in the cause, just as she had been before she'd been captured. They had been willing to risk their lives for her, and she...

Well she had given her heart to a vampire, the oldest son in the royal family no less, the heir to the throne. They had been willing to die for her while she had been falling in love with one of their greatest enemies. She thought of the prince as a monster, and because she loved him she had also come to accept the fact that she must be one too.

"I suspected," he murmured. "You can't blame yourself Aria, it was an awful time. Things were warped and wrong in there. It's not your fault that you trusted him. Of course you did, it was frightening, and you became confused. He had a month to manipulate you, to make you think that you could believe in him, that you could love him."

"Oh Max," she breathed, wishing that the explanation was as simple as that, but she knew it wasn't. The prince had not twisted her; he had not used her terror and confusion against her. He had been kind and caring, and he had needed her, she knew that. Though he'd had a fiancée the whole time, at the very least she knew that she'd been a little bit special to him. But she still should have fought against her feelings more, he was her enemy, he would always be her enemy, and they'd never had a chance at a future. She had known all of that, and yet she had still offered him her blood with no reservations, and no fear.

She had given him her heart willingly also. She hated to pop Max's bubble, but he couldn't go about thinking such things. He had to know that she hadn't been corrupted in there, but a willing, even *eager*, participant. He had to know that she was a horrible person. He had to know these things so that he would stop looking at her like that, so that he would understand she could never care for him the same way that he cared for her.

"I'm sorry Max," she whispered. "But that's not what happened. He didn't manipulate me, he didn't corrupt me. He was kind to me, he took care of me. I may have been his blood slave, but he only treated me as such when it was absolutely necessary. I would like to say that I hadn't come to care for him, that I had remained loyal to you and everyone here, but I can't. I loved him Max..." She broke off, unable to speak through the grief that clawed at her. "I still love him," she choked out.

He stared at her for a moment, his eyes wide in disbelief, and then he shook his head rapidly. His sandy blond hair fell across his forehead curling around his bright eyes. "But don't you see Aria that *is* how he twisted you. He knew that you'd always had nothing, that your life had been hard. He knew that by being kind, by giving you the things that you'd never had, you would come to rely on him, trust him, and perhaps even convince yourself you cared for him. That way it would be more fun when he destroyed you, it's why he never told you he was engaged."

Aria's fingernails clawed into the edge of the river bank as she grasped it. She tried to believe Max's words. Maybe, just maybe, she could move on if she believed them, but she couldn't. Yes, the prince had kept his fiancée from her, yes he had been dishonest, and yes he had broken her heart, but something between them *had* been real. There had been a strange connection between them from the very beginning. Max knew that the prince was blind; he didn't know that whenever the prince was near her, he could see again.

And though the prince had omitted things about his life, she knew he hadn't been lying about the fact that he could only see when he was around her. The fact that he could see her was the reason that he had claimed her as his first blood slave. No, Max didn't know about that, and as far as she was concerned no one ever would, not even the prince's brother Jack. That was one secret that would stay completely between the two of them. It was the one secret that she clung to; the one idea that made her believe it hadn't all been a lie. It was the only thing that helped to ease her self-disgust just a little.

Although she knew she would never see or feel him again, and even though he had hurt her so badly, she needed to believe that he had cared for her, at least a little bit. It probably wasn't the best idea for her to cling to that notion, not when she had to let him go, but she couldn't help it. Right now it was the only thing that was getting her through the days.

"I don't think so Max."

"I do," he replied with more confidence than she had. "And one day you will realize it too. You just need time for his psychological games to wear off, and when they do, I'll be here."

Aria shook her head. "No Max..."

Her words broke off as he clasped hold of her chin, turning her so that she had to face him. He wiped the tears from her face. Tears she hadn't even known she was crying. "Yes Aria."

Before she could react, he was leaning forward and kissing her. Aria started in surprise, she didn't know what to do or how to respond, but before she could do anything he was already pulling away from her. She could only sit and stare at him as he smiled back at her. "Just thought it was time for our second kiss."

She couldn't have disagreed more, but she didn't say so. She was being selfish by not telling him that, but she had already lost so much in the past couple of months, she couldn't bear to lose Max's friendship as well. However, once he realized who she truly was, how little she deserved his love, he would turn against her. "We should be going," she managed to choke out.

Nodding, he quickly climbed to his feet wiping the dirt and mud off his pants as he went. Aria listened to the familiar sounds of the forest, *her* forest as she followed him. She had always taken solace and refuge within these thick woods, but she hadn't been able to find either of those things as of late.

~

LEANING against the wall of the cave Aria stared out the entrance. In the shadows of the evening, she could just barely make out the figures of a few guards, but she only saw them because she knew that they were there. If she hadn't known, she never would have been able to see them amongst their strategic hiding spots. The caves were good shelter, but without fair warning that an attack was coming, it was easy to get trapped within the thick walls. There were many escape routes throughout the underground system, but there were just as many dead ends.

She glanced behind her, but the cave was dark. The fires were lit much further beneath the earth, where they couldn't be seen from the woods. She didn't fool herself into thinking that she was alone out here; her father had people watching her like a hawk since she'd been taken, but at least she had a little sense of peace and tranquility. Well, that was until she felt William coming.

She turned as her twin emerged from the dark recesses of the cave. She would know him anywhere and often felt him coming before he actually arrived. He leaned against the wall opposite her, his arms folded over his chest as he gazed at her. They both had the same bright blue eyes, the same dark auburn hair. Though they'd come from two different eggs, they were even more similar than most identical twins. Right down to their quick tempers and impulsive actions.

Those impulsive actions were what led her to be captured and subsequently made into a blood slave, and though she'd like to say that they were both more thoughtful now, she knew she'd be lying. The only thing that had changed was she was sadder and more mature than she had been before going into the palace, and William was angrier. He blamed himself for not being with her that day, even though he'd been injured and unable to accompany her on the hunt. He hated the vampires for taking her, and he especially hated the prince for claiming her as a blood slave.

She had tried to explain to all of them that she hadn't been abused, that it was only her heart that had been maimed, but none of them believed her. She supposed it didn't help that she was more like the walking dead than a living person since her return. She most certainly wasn't the same girl that had been taken from the woods, and they blamed the prince for that. They didn't understand that he had saved her from a fate far worse than the one she'd actually experienced. It had been another vampire that had claimed her originally, if it hadn't been for the prince far worse things would have been done to her. Whereas they felt she'd been tortured, she knew she'd been quite lucky.

"Do you think you'll ever fall in love?" she questioned.

He turned toward her, his eyes bright in the night, his dark eyebrows quirked upward as he studied her. "Is that what you think you were?"

She was silent as she thought over her next words. She had never kept anything from William, they had always shared everything, but he had been so angry lately that she was frightened her words might send him over the edge. She couldn't lie to him though. "Yes."

He swallowed heavily as he ran a hand through his shaggy hair. She could tell he was trying to keep hold of his temper, struggling to hide the vehemence behind his emotion from her. "Aria, things happened in there, things I can't even begin to imagine..."

"Don't William. Max may choose to believe that, but you know better. You know me, you know who I am. Do you really think I don't know what I felt in there?"

"I believe that you *think* you do." Aria's hands fisted in frustration; it seemed that everyone thought she didn't know her own feelings. But she supposed that if it were William telling her these things, she wouldn't believe them either. "And no, I don't think I will ever fall in love."

"Oh."

He moved away from the wall, throwing his arm casually around her shoulders he pulled her against his side. He grinned down at her; she couldn't help but grin back at him. For the first time in their lives he may not understand her, but he would always love her. No matter what. She dropped her head to his chest and wrapped her arm around his waist. She listened to the sound of his heart as they stared out at the night. She was so absorbed in the reassuring beat that it took her a few moments to realize that all of the animals, and insects, had gone silent.

Aria lifted her head slowly, her heart thumped wildly as she gazed out at the darkness. She searched for the guards amongst the trees; she spotted their prone figures amid the darkness. "William," she whispered.

"I know. Come on."

He pushed her deeper into the cave, with his hand on her back, as they made their way swiftly through the familiar terrain. The guards still hadn't raised the alarm, a low pitched whistle that could easily blend in with the chirruping of the insects, but Aria strained to hear it. It had to be coming soon. "Hurry!" A sense of doom descended over her as her breath came faster.

Her hand clenched upon William's, when they were far enough from the entrance, they broke into a run. Their feet flew over the rock of the cave floor. They might already be too late if the vampires were already upon them. With the vampire's exceptional eyesight in the dark, and their rapid speed, it would be almost impossible for her and William to escape. They took a side tunnel on the right, ducking low as the ceiling became lower. William turned back and grabbed hold of one of the heavy iron gates that had been built into the wall.

"The guards!" she hissed, grabbing hold of his arm before he could close the gate.

"It's too late for them Aria."

Horror filled her as the low pitched warning whistle echoed through the caves. William froze for a moment; the gate was still partly open when she sensed, more than heard, something approaching. William effectively sealed the guards out as he closed the gate as quietly as possible. There were many other tunnels leading through here. It could take awhile for the vampires to find the right tunnel, and the gate should buy them enough time to try and escape.

They retreated, moving as quickly as they could through the stooped tunnel. Aria's heart pounded rapidly in her chest, a crushing sense of time running out seized hold of her as something large and heavy slammed into the gate, rattling it within its frame.

# CHAPTER TWO

ARIA WAS PANTING for air as they raced forward. They were running on instinct and memory alone, too disturbed by what was behind them to grab one of the unlit torches from the walls surrounding them. William led her around another turn, pausing long enough to reach back and slide a gate shut. They weren't far from the main room now. She stumbled over a loose stone, and her ankle rolled out beneath her as he pulled her forward. A muted cry escaped her but she hurried on, refusing to be hindered by the throbbing that raced up her leg.

The tunnel began to narrow as William slid another gate home. As they maneuvered another turn, the fire of the main room became visible and she could hear the faint sounds of laughter. Aria's heart hammered, she could barely breathe. She had never felt claustrophobic within the tunnels before, now she felt like a caged rat running aimlessly forward. If they got out of this she swore she would never return to these caves. Then again, they could never return to them anyway, they would never be safe again.

They had been discovered.

William and Aria stumbled into the main hall. Everyone became silent as William spun around to push another gate shut. "They're here!" Aria informed them.

There were a good hundred people in the room; panic claimed over half of them. Screams rang out, children began to cry. Though they had run drills, and practiced for this sort of thing, it had never happened before. Aria was dismayed and horrified to see the chaos that promptly took over. Her mouth dropped as people began to run about, trying to gather as many of their things as possible. Thankfully, some kept a level head long enough to shut the three gates that blocked the tunnels from the main room.

She wished that her father, or Daniel, were here. They would have an easier time at keeping everyone calm, but they had gone to meet with another group of rebels about a mile away in another set of caves. "Everyone! Everyone! You have to calm down!" She raced into the center of the room, holding her hands up as she tried to calm the fray. No one paid her any attention as they began to push and shove their way toward the only remaining exit. "Wait!" she cried, trying to stop them before they trampled each other and lost their only chance at escape.

Max grabbed hold of her arm, pulling her free of the crushing bodies. Thrusting her behind him, she was pinned between his body and the cave wall. Aria grasped his shirt as he pressed against her, trying to protect her from the jostling and shoving.

"Everyone calm down!" His voice was louder than normal, but not so loud that it would bounce down the tunnels, and not so loud that it caused anyone to hesitate for more than a moment. "Damn it!"

His frustration was apparent in the constriction of his muscles, and his fisted hands. He turned toward her, bracing one hand against the wall by her head as he fought and pushed against the mass of bodies. Grabbing hold of her arm, he pulled her against him as he began to shove his way back through the disarray, fighting against the seemingly endless sea of people. She searched for William, but she couldn't see him amongst the wave of bodies.

As they finally broke free she struggled to get oxygen into her abused lungs. William was suddenly before her, he thrust her bow and a quiver of arrows into her hands. "We're going to have to find another way out."

The tunnel behind them, the one everyone was shoving through, was the only one that didn't eventually meet back up with the main tunnel they had just left. There were ways outside, through other tunnels, but there was a chance that the vampires were already in one of those tunnels. To open one of the gates back up and go into one of those tunnels was a huge risk. It was something they had never planned on having to do.

She glanced back at the exit tunnel, it was jammed full of bodies pushing and shoving at each other. In the drills they had run, most people were supposed to be halfway through the tunnel by now. Panic had hindered things; she was certain there were people on the ground in there being trampled by the mob.

"We have to help them."

She took a step toward them but William grabbed hold of her arm and pulled her back sharply. "There is no helping them now Aria; we have to get out of here before we're trapped. We have to go."

"The people," she whispered.

"Will be fine, they have the safe exit, remember?" he retorted. "Come on."

He pulled her back toward the gate that they had entered the cavern through. "We just came through there," she breathed.

"There are three gates already closed between us and the main hall. It will be the safest one."

His long fingers worked deftly over the locks, swiftly throwing them open. Three other men and a woman gathered with them. They had apparently decided to throw their chances in with them, rather than the crushing mass of people on the other side. Aria didn't know who they were, but the people within the caves changed often. Most of the rebels relocated constantly, preferring to stay on the move rather than remain cooped up in one place. It was a theory that her family had also stuck to, but her father had stayed here for far longer than normal. Aria knew it was because of her. He wanted her to rest and recuperate in one place, and maybe even have some sense of stability for once in her life.

She'd hated being stuck here, and now she knew why. She felt much safer when they were constantly moving, felt much safer outside in the woods she knew so well. Yet, they had spent so much time over the years running in and out of the cave systems that she knew most of them by heart. She always felt like a caged animal when she was within the caves. She'd wanted to make her dad happy though, especially when he was obviously worried about her, so she hadn't complained about staying. She wished she had now. The caves would have been raided, even if they hadn't been here, but she couldn't help but feel like this was somehow her fault. That somehow she had brought them here.

"Come on," Max said as he seized hold of her hand.

They plunged back into the black tunnels. The darkness enveloped them; she could barely make out the back of Max's head as she strained to see. They couldn't use any of the torches though, that was just begging to be caught and killed, or worse, she could be re-captured and brought back to whatever horrible fate awaited her at the palace. She had the distinct feeling that if she was brought back to the palace, it would not go over well. In fact, although the prince was engaged, she thought she would be made to pay dearly for her escape. She knew how badly he hated to be disobeyed and her escape had been the ultimate defiance. He would punish her for it. Or he wouldn't even care that she was back, and let her go to whoever tried to claim her this time.

She shuddered at the thought. Her hand clung to the strap of the bow and quiver slung over her back. They were her specialty; she could shoot an arrow better than anyone else. She just wasn't going to be able to do it in these restricted confines, and from the direction William was heading, she knew that it was about to get a lot more compact in here. She hated this route through the caverns, but it was the one that made the most sense right now. It would be harder for the vampires to navigate through here also, and at this point the other tunnel options led to a waterfall. It was a beautiful view, but the sound of rushing water blocked out the noise of their pursuers, and they were relying on their sense of hearing most right now. The rocks were also slippery, and climbing them under the best of circumstances was risky enough, without adding the bonus obstacle of rushing.

William took a sharp right. The tunnel began to climb steeply upward. They were heading toward the back of the mountain, and what had once been an old coal mining operation, or so she had been told. Aria hated the old coal mines; they were creepy, hazardous, and filthy. Thankfully William took a left and began to climb toward the other side of the mountain. The air became easier to breathe, although the walls were still snug against them, she didn't feel quite as pinned in.

Max's hand tightened around hers. She was grateful for his reassuring presence, his solid strength and warmth as he led her hastily forward. William stopped suddenly, causing the woman to roughly bump into him. They stood silently, straining to hear anything within the dark, damp space. They were only a hundred feet from the end of the tunnel, only a hundred feet from freedom, or certain death.

"We're going to have to move fast. Stay low and head straight for the woods. If we get separated for some reason we'll meet up again at the south edge of the lake," William instructed. "If we can't get to the south edge of the lake, we'll meet at the banquet tree."

The banquet tree was something she and William had discovered when they were children. It was simply an extremely large apple tree, but it had seemed massive and fantastic to them as they spent hours climbing its immense limbs, and gorging themselves on the apples they picked from it. For a couple weeks every year they'd had an ample supply of fruit, and aching bellies but it had always been worth it.

They were also the only ones who knew where the tree was. They had brought the fruit back to the camps, willingly sharing it with everyone, but they had never revealed its location, and now that she thought about it, she didn't think anyone had ever asked. It was as if they had all understood that she and William required a place of their own, and allowed them to keep it.

Aria's hand tightened around Max's. She understood that William was mostly concerned with her safety, but she couldn't lose Max. He had risked his life for hers; he had sacrificed himself for her. She would not take the chance that they were separated now. She thought that she should feel more guilt about possibly losing the others but she didn't, not when it came to her brother and her friend. Their world was cruel, brutal, and for most people it was every man for themselves, except for the few people that ran in somewhat larger circles like she did.

It was nice to have friends, and family that she could rely on, that she could trust with her life. The downfall of it all was the grief that would come with the loss of any one of them. She had been lucky so far.

William rushed forward, leading the way as they raced through the dark, up the slope, toward the unknown.

They plunged into the night. Aria inhaled large, greedy gulps of the fresh air, relieved to be free of the confining space of the caves. They were almost a hundred feet from the cave exit when the screaming pierced through the rapid beat of her heart in her ears. She froze, sadness coiling through her as she turned back around. They were higher up on the mountainside, staring down across the way. The lake was beneath them, gleaming in the moonlight that reflected off of it. Across the lake was the exit from the escape tunnel, hidden within a copse of trees.

The exit had been selected because it was the farthest point from the main entrance, and well concealed. It was also where the screams were coming from. Aria's mouth went dry; she took a step forward as revulsion and dread coursed through her. Across the lake she could see people scattering in every direction, fleeing as they tried to escape the monsters pursuing them.

Aria couldn't fully comprehend the carnage before her. They had to do something. *Now*! She darted forward, determined to get down there and help those people. Max seized hold of her arm, pulling her back. She strained against him as he started to pull her toward the woods.

"We have to help!" she protested.

He grabbed hold of her other arm, holding her before him as he shook her slightly. "There is nothing we can do Aria, we have to go! We have to go *now*!"

She tried to fight him, but he kept his stern hold. "We can't just leave them!"

His eyes were dark, sad, broken in the moonlight. "It's too late for them." Her gaze turned back to the spectacle below her, she couldn't abandon them. "It's how we were captured before Aria; you cannot heedlessly run in again."

His words froze her, she couldn't move as her heart labored to pump blood through her suddenly frigid body. It *was* how they had been captured before, it had been her fault that they had been taken, and she couldn't allow that to happen again. Her gaze wandered hopelessly over to William. He stood at the edge of the forest, waiting impatiently for them. The others had already fled into the darkness. If she went down there again, if she tried to interfere again, they would follow her, and they would be caught.

There was nothing that any of them could do to help the people being hunted now. There was no way to stop the massacre raging below them, no way to silence the screams. There was no one to save them if they were captured again; no one would come to rescue them as Jack had blown his cover amongst his family. The royal family knew Jack was a traitor now, and wouldn't welcome him back unless it was to torture and destroy him. They might not even be captured this time; they could just be slaughtered outright.

Max gently pulled her back and away from the scene before them. "Hurry!" William urged.

"It will be ok, Aria. It will be ok." Max wrapped his hand around the back of her head, pulling her close for a brief moment before tugging her toward the woods. They plunged into the darkness, moving speedily through the dense forest. William led the way, taking a zigzagging route that wound rapidly toward the banquet tree.

Aria felt numb, hollow. The screams of the tortured followed her even after they were out of earshot. She fell against the large tree, clinging to one of its branches as she wheezed for air that she couldn't quite get. Her legs buckled, she fell to her knees before their childhood tree. So many dreams and plans and hopes had grown from this spot.

Those dreams were gone now and in their place were bleak hopelessness and the echoing screams of the innocent. What once was a place of safety and shelter was now tainted by loss and suffering. Yet, beneath all of that there was something else, something new rising up to course through her, a feeling she couldn't identify amidst all of the agony and confusion tearing her apart. For a moment, she didn't know what it was that was consuming her. And then, she did.

It was hatred.

It was pure and simple *hate*. She hated this world of cruelty, hated the monsters that had created it. She hated it with everything that she had and was. And she hated the monster that had done this to her, the creature that had stomped all over her heart, making her weaker, making her a broken shell of the person she had once been. And now, well now that shell was filling up again. That shell was infuriated and twisted and so hate filled that she could barely breathe through its fiery consumption.

The prince, she *hated* the prince, she realized.

There would be no more grieving for him, there would be no more wondering and heartache. What had passed between them was the past. It was over. She would forget it, she would move on, and if their paths ever happened to cross again. She *would* kill him.

# CHAPTER THREE

"There was a raid."

Braith silently pondered Caleb's words as the tailor moved deliberately around him. The man finally had stopped mumbling to himself, and although he continued to work, Braith knew he was listening raptly to the conversation. "And?" Braith prodded.

"She was not amongst the captured."

"The dead?"

"No. The soldiers know that she is to be brought back here alive, if she's caught. That they all are."

Braith shrugged, disliking the feel of the coat he wore. "No matter the orders, there are always casualties in war," he murmured. He expected Caleb to leave after delivering the news. Even twisted, brutal Caleb didn't like to be around him for any length of time anymore. No one did. Braith's temper had become volatile, his fury and paths of destruction were well known, and feared, amongst the residents of the palace.

A lot of blood had stained his hands over the past two months; he had consumed more blood in the past eight weeks than he had in the past eight years. But it was not enough; it would never be enough to bury the hatred festering inside of him. His murderous rampage had died down, but only because he had calmed enough to realize that the deaths of innocent people didn't ease his rage and didn't make him forget as much as he had hoped it would. Now he just consumed mass quantities of blood, but most of the time the people survived it now.

"Is there more?" he demanded impatiently of his brother.

Caleb cleared his throat. "She was not amongst the dead, and she was not amongst the captured, but she was there."

Braith's head slowly came up as he turned toward his brother. He couldn't see Caleb, darkness ruled his life once more, but he could smell the faint hint of excitement that rolled off of him. He stood for a protracted moment, stunned by Caleb's words. There had been no sign of her since she'd left here, and though he could have found her at any time, he refused to lower himself by going after her, by making her think that he desired her back, because he didn't. She had betrayed him after all; he wanted nothing more to do with the traitorous bitch.

And yet he felt a moment of apprehension rock through him. While he would like her punished for her treachery, would like her to suffer for what she had done to him, did he truly want her dead? Did he want her back here where she would be tortured and punished for her treachery? He had believed so, he had wanted it to *be* so, but now that his troops had stumbled across her, now that they were hot on her heels, he didn't know what he would do if she was recaptured. She would be tortured, beaten, and eventually killed. She would be branded a traitor, and she would be dealt with as such. It would be a brutal punishment.

If he really wanted her back, then he would have gone after her himself and brought her back here by now. But even though he hated her, even though she had sliced him deeply, and he would like for her to suffer as badly as he had upon first discovering her gone, he had to admit that he didn't want her dead.

In all the time since she'd been gone, it was the first time that he actually realized this fact. He coveted her blood, he yearned to taste her and see her again, and *he* was going to be the one that made her pay for her deceitfulness, not his brother or his father. His jaw clenched as he grasped the lapels on the jacket he wore. The hated jacket. The tailor made a faint sound of protest as he stepped down from the dais he had been standing upon, ignoring the annoying gnat of a man.

"How do you know she was there?" he growled.

"One of our people spotted her; it was why they went in when they did. They were hoping to capture her."

"Went in?"

"They were in a group of caves, apparently well engineered caves with a series of tunnels and gates throughout them. The caves were discovered last week, but they were going to wait until they knew where all of the exits were before raiding them. Our guards got a little overexcited when they spotted her and jumped the gun."

*Caves*, she was living in caves. She had spoken about her woods, and her forest, with such reverence that he had assumed she'd return directly to them as soon as she was free. Instead, she was living in *caves*, hidden beneath the earth, trapped beneath mounds of dirt and rock. It made no sense to him, but what made even less sense was the fact that he even remotely cared where she was living or what she was doing.

He had moved on with his life, he now owned several blood slaves, and though none of them were her, he found he did enjoy them. They made him forget for a little bit, they made it not so difficult to get through the days. Unlike Arianna, these slaves were far more pliant, and far less defiant. He was getting married in a matter of months, granted he couldn't stand the woman, but he need only have a male heir with her and then he wouldn't have to have anything to do with her again. He hadn't planned on marrying the woman, no matter what his father had arranged, but he was resigned to it now. For once, he hadn't intended to do his duty as the eldest son. Not until Arianna had abandoned him, running away with his brother and another blood slave.

After that, all he had longed for was to forget. There were even times during the day when he almost did forget, brief moments when he found a little reprieve from his memories in the copious amounts of blood. Those moments never lasted though, and there was a part of him that hated himself for what he was doing, but he knew that with enough blood, and enough time, he would eventually forget her. Eventually Arianna would die, she was human, and she lived a perilous life. It was only a matter of time before it happened, he would know when that time came, and he had thought that he would feel relief when it did.

He wasn't so sure now.

"Was there any sign of Jericho?"

Resentment boiled through him at the mention of his youngest brother, the sibling he had trusted and liked the most, and the one that had betrayed him the deepest. The one that had *taken* Arianna from him. Though he doubted she had put up any fight. In fact, he was fairly certain that despite her vows of love, and her promises to never leave him, she had run eagerly through the tunnel once it had been revealed to her. She was a fickle bitch after all, or at least that's what he had come to believe. Why else would she vow to love him forever and then leave him the very next morning?

And Jericho had become enemy number one now. Braith may not personally destroy Arianna, but he thought he would have a try at Jericho.

"They didn't see Jericho there, but I'm sure he was nearby. After all, he betrayed us for her, she must mean something to him."

Jericho had said that he was here to rescue Arianna because her father was the leader of the rebels. Jericho had come here for her because he was one of the few that could get her free. That's what he'd claimed, but Braith had a tough time believing anything that had come out of his brother's mouth during those days. His brother had also said that he wouldn't do anything without consulting Braith first, and then he had disappeared the next day.

In fact, he thought that Caleb was right, that Jericho did feel more for Arianna than just friendship and loyalty, why else would he have taken her like he had? Braith had never revealed to Caleb, or his father, Arianna's true history. There was no point in doing so, she was gone now, and there was no way to use her against her family anymore.

"There was a different man with her."

Braith's mouth curved in a sneer. "Was there," he said sardonically. How many men did the little bitch have? He speculated angrily. First there had been the blood slave, Max, then his brother, and now some other mystery man. His fingers twitched into a fist, he fought against the surge of bloodlust that tore through him. He was desperate to bury his fangs in something in order to try and forget the anger raging through him.

"Yes. They have no idea who it was, but it wasn't Jericho and it wasn't the other blood slave."

A muscle in his cheek began to twitch in aggravation; he felt his temper starting to unravel. He had thought Arianna a sweet innocent who had brought light back into his life. He was beginning to learn that nothing could be farther from the truth.

"I see." But he didn't see, and he wondered why he didn't go after her and drag her back here kicking and screaming. Why he didn't go after her, destroy her family, smash her rebel cause, and hunt down his treasonous brother and make them all pay. Pacing away, he tore the jacket off, suddenly feeling claustrophobic within the material. The tailor made a strangled sound of despair as the material ripped, but Braith didn't care. "Have they brought any blood slaves back?" he demanded.

"Yes, they are leading them onto the stage now."

Braith nodded, he grabbed his cane and hefted it into his hands. Keegan, his ever faithful wolf and seeing dog, yawned before rising to his feet. His claws clicked against the wood floor as he walked beside Braith. "Let's go."

Caleb hesitated for only moment before falling into step beside him. Braith was used to the darkness, used to navigating it; he didn't require any assistance as he moved through the hallways of the palace. The cane clicked off the floor, but it was Keegan that always alerted him to any new obstacle that may have been placed in the way. With a subtle pressure against his leg Keegan could steer him easily one way or the other.

Braith swiftly made his way down to the stage that held the future blood slaves. Though he was before the stage his vision didn't come back to him as it had the day that Arianna had been on the auction block. He'd been unable to move at the sight of her, unable to believe that he could actually *see* anything again, let alone this frightened, dirty, bedraggled girl that was everything he disliked about a woman.

She was not round, she was not voluptuous, she smelled far from decent, and yet he had *seen* her. She was the first thing he had witnessed in over a hundred years. And slowly, over the time he spent with her, she had become infinitely beautiful to him. Yes she was defiant, harsh, far too skinny for his taste, and not beautiful in the classical sense, but she was also strong, sweet, innocent, and unbelievably breathtaking. He had come to care greatly for her, until he had realized that it was all a lie. That she was in fact none of those things, and was instead a cunning, manipulative shrew.

He stared in the direction of the stage once more, but still nothing popped out at him. No other women appeared to him, no one else gave him vision again. "Is there anyone up there that could be her family?"

Caleb was silent for a few moments. "Not that I can see. I'm going to grab a few of them, I'm sure they'll eventually tell us more. And if they don't," Braith heard Caleb's shrug of indifference. "I will enjoy trying to make them talk."

Braith stood silently, listening as blood slaves were brought forth and auctioned off. Caleb claimed four of them. Braith briefly contemplated taking a few more of his own, but decided against it. He had enough, for now.

He turned away, if there was anything to learn, Caleb would do it. He made his way back toward the palace, wondering where Jericho had been during the raid, wondering who it was that she had been with. *Another* man? Just how many damn men did she have in her life? He tried to tell himself that he didn't care about the answer to that question, but he knew he did. He could not deny it. The bitch had betrayed him, and now she was running free, wrapping even more men around her devious little finger. He hated her for making him one of those men.

He easily made his way through the crowd, his mind churning. Resentment simmered hotly inside of him. He needed a new plan. He couldn't simply sit here and allow her to get away with everything that she had done. He couldn't allow his brother to sit amongst the humans, laughing about how he had managed to deceive his eldest brother, and his family.

Braith had made the decision to let them be, he was now beginning to rethink that decision. They should pay for what they had done, and he could make them do that. They may be able to avoid his men, but they couldn't avoid him.

Especially *her*.

~

RAIN DRIPPED MELODICALLY onto the makeshift tent. The piece of canvas offered little protection against the elements, but Aria didn't care. The air was refreshing and gave her a feel of freedom after all the time spent cooped up in the caves. It helped to ease the sense of claustrophobia that still haunted her, but it did little to wash away the persistent screams that had woken her every night for the past week.

She could retreat to the shelter of the caves, but she knew that she wouldn't. She couldn't bring herself to go back in them now, if ever. So instead she sat in silence, listening to the plop of the water upon the tent. Max and William had been her constant companions since the night of the raid. William would go out once in awhile to gather food but Max wouldn't leave her side.

He moved closer to her, dropping a blanket around her shoulders. His hands lingered upon her for a moment, and she didn't shrug him away. She found she needed his comfort and his loyal, unwavering love right now.

She leaned into him, resting against his legs. "You have to get some sleep," he told her.

"I will." They both knew she lied, but he didn't argue with her.

When she shivered, he wrapped his arms around her. Pulling her against his chest he cradled her gently. Though her heart did not thump with excitement, as it had when the prince touched her, his strong embrace was comforting. She felt safe in his arms, cherished. No, he didn't affect her as the prince had, but he was a good man, he loved her, and he would do anything for her.

Maybe one day she would love him too, even if that day couldn't be now. Now she just wanted to feel something other than resentment and despair. Now she simply wanted to sit with her friend, content in his arms, as she listened to the rain fall. "It smells good," she whispered.

Max nodded, nuzzling her hair for a moment. "Yes."

Aria closed her eyes, concentrating on the beat of his heart. The prince hadn't had a heartbeat; in fact he hadn't had a heart at all as far as she was concerned. But Max did, and he wore it on his sleeve. He pulled the blanket more firmly around her, the heat of his body, and the melodious splatter of the rain lulled her into a fitful sleep.

When she awoke again, the sky was just beginning to glow; the birds hadn't even begun to sing yet. She stared silently at the growing dawn against the walls of the tent. Max's arm was wrapped around her waist, William was curled against the back wall snoring. She slipped from beneath his embrace and moved to the edge of the tent to pull the flap aside. It was going to be a warm day; the air was already muggy with heat. She sighed softly and slipped from the tent. She planned to bathe, and then perhaps do some hunting with Max and William.

She gathered some of her clothes and scooped up her bow and quiver. Max and William were still sleeping; the sun had just poked over the horizon as she dropped the flap back into place. She moved through the forest, winding her way toward the river near where they were camped. She knew she shouldn't be doing this on her own, that she should wake someone to come with her, but she needed some time alone to try and sort through the multitude of emotions swarming her.

She quickly made her way to the edge of the river. She would have preferred the lake, but after the raid they had moved far from the caves, settling in a new area of the forest. It would be awhile before they went back near the lake again. Reaching the river, she stripped and plunged into the chilly water. Not for the first time, she missed the hot water of the palace, and the delightful spray of the shower. The lake had been tolerably warm and comfortable, but the river was fresh water from the mountains, and it didn't warm up.

Aria bathed as quickly as she could, her teeth chattering as she shivered the whole time. She was glad to escape the frigid water, glad to put some clothes back on so that she could warm up. Grabbing her bow and quiver, she slung the quiver onto her back. The sun was breaking over the mountains, its bright rays lit up the forest around her as they filtered through the leafy bowers. She stood for a moment, her head tilted back to allow its warmth to caress her, to soothe her, if only just a little.

She didn't know how long she stood there, but the snap of a twig pulled her away from the healing sunlight back to the world around her. Aria concentrated, listening as she heard another faint snap. Moving behind a tree, she drew an arrow from her quiver as she knelt. She didn't have to wait long before a buck wandered out of the woods, heading toward the river. Aria admired him, but even though he was a gorgeous animal, he would also provide enough meat for the encampment to last a few days. He would feed the hungry children, and her, she realized as her stomach rumbled eagerly in anticipation.

She was about to let the arrow fly when she felt it. These woods were engrained in her soul, a part of her, and she knew when a predator was near. The hair on the back of her neck stood up, a chill crept down her back before seeping through her limbs. She froze, she couldn't breathe. She didn't move. She was nervous that moving would only trigger an attack. She knew when an animal was close to its end, but this time she was not the hunter, and it was *her* end she feared. She was certain that there was the deadliest kind of predator near her right now.

Slowly, ever so slowly, she turned to face the creature stalking her, watching her. She spotted him almost instantly. Braith stood amongst the trees, his black hair highlighted by the rising sun, was a stark contrast to the greenery surrounding him. Light reflected off of the dark glasses he wore to cover his striking eyes, but even so she could feel the heat of his gaze as it raked over her. Her heart knocked against her ribs, it flipped and beat and pounded in a rapid pace that left her immobile and breathless. He was just as magnificent, dark and powerful as she remembered, but seeing him here, in her world, she also realized just how wild and untamed he was. Just how dangerous and lethal he could be.

Excitement strummed through her, for a brief moment she was consumed with the urge to run to him, to throw her arms around him, to bury herself in his strong embrace and shut out all the misery of the world like only he could make her do. For a brief moment, all of the joy and wonder she had ever experienced with him in the palace rapidly flooded back to her. She had been terrified in that palace, lost and adrift in a world that she didn't know and would never understand. But she had also been the happiest she'd ever been in her life. She'd been foolish, and naïve. And she had been in love.

Her arm wavered on the bow, dropping it momentarily lower; she could feel the hot press of tears burning her eyes. He was breathtaking, he looked amazing, and he was *here*. He had finally come for her. Though she hated to admit it, there had been a part of her that had craved this. A part that had pined for him to come for her, to take her away from all of this desolation and pain, and keep her safe and love her. She hated that part of herself, tried to deny its existence, but it had always been there, hoping, waiting, praying, and now he was finally *here*.

But it was obvious that he hadn't come just to see her.

She could see that fact in the rigid set of his jaw and the tension in his broad shoulders. She could sense it in the rage that radiated from his stiff body. He was here, but he hadn't come for a good reason. Aria swallowed heavily, trepidation trickled through her as she realized that he was truly furious right now. She could feel the tremendous amount of fury directed solely at her. Well that was good, because she was pretty pissed at him too.

She didn't know why he had finally come after her, but from the look of him it appeared that he wanted to rip her throat out. Narrowing her eyes, she clenched her jaw as she lifted the bow higher once more, leveling it right at the spot of his non-beating heart. Yes, he had finally come for her and it was obvious that one of them would not be walking away from this encounter.

# CHAPTER FOUR

BRAITH STUDIED her for a lengthy moment. He had almost forgotten how astonishing it was to see her, and everything around her. The forest came alive with her in it; the colors were vivid, sharp to eyes so accustomed to darkness. Though the woods were beautiful, they were nothing compared to *her*.

Her face was thinner and more mature than the last time he had seen her. The youthful chubbiness of her cheeks had again vanished in the face of malnourishment. Her eyes were a bright sapphire blue that rivaled the beautiful sky behind her. There was a wisdom and maturity in her gaze, a broken air that seemed to enshroud her, but hadn't been there the last time he'd seen her. He didn't know what had happened to her over the past couple of months, but she appeared older, and far more wounded than he recalled.

Her hair flowed around her shoulders and back; its wetness caused it to be darker than its normal fiery auburn color that had always captivated him. She was far cleaner now than the first time he'd seen her, but she was back in the boyish, ugly clothes again. Clothes that hid a figure that had once been lush, but was now lean again. Though she was thinner than he liked her, he couldn't deny her simple, sweet beauty.

He saw the emotions that flashed over her face, the hope, the joy, and for a moment something he almost believed could have been love. But they were gone so rapidly that he wasn't even entirely sure he'd seen them. Tears shimmered in her eyes; her hand wavered on the bow as it dropped down. He'd almost forgotten how convincing her phony emotions could be. He recalled the night she had begged him not to kill the other blood slave she'd been captured with. She had been so sincere, had sworn that Max was nothing more than a friend to her. Braith no longer believed that, he believed nothing of what she had told him. He didn't know the girl before him, but he did know that she was not the girl he'd thought she was. She never had been.

He had come here to bring her back, to make her pay for her betrayal. Now all he would like to do was destroy her himself. Her arm wavered but the hand that had been going to drop the bow now raised it back up, leveling it at his heart. He had no doubt she would let the arrow fly, just as he had no concern that it would actually hit him.

Just as he had no doubt that he would get his hands upon her, and she would pay.

"Arianna."

Her full mouth pinched, her eyebrows were tight over her narrow nose. "Prince."

He moved away from the tree he had been leaning against, taking a step toward her. Even with the bow and arrow in her hands, he could get to her, reach her within a moment. Have her back in his arms again, her sweet blood back in his mouth. She had given it to him willingly last time, and he had almost killed her in his eagerness to consume it. Now he was going to taste it again, and he didn't give a shit if she gave it freely or not. He found himself relishing the idea of taking it from her forcefully, of making her hurt as bad as she had caused him to.

"Have you come to take me back then?" she inquired roughly.

"No."

She swallowed heavily, her chin tilted up a notch. He hadn't forgotten about her defiance, her willfulness, but he didn't find it as charming as he once had. In fact, it was aggravating the hell out of him right now. She should be cowering, trembling with fear. She had to know that she would

not survive this meeting, and yet she didn't show one ounce of trepidation.

Recklessly fearless, it was how she had described herself and her
brother. And it was true. She was possibly looking her death in the eye,
but she wasn't going to back down from him. She wasn't going to cower
or beg for mercy. She was going to stand there and meet him head on,
and she was going to fire that arrow. Of that he was certain; he just had to
be prepared for it.

"To kill me then?" she inquired, her voice far steadier then he had
thought it should be.

"Perhaps," he murmured. He had planned to take her back, to make
her pay, but then she would be killed, and looking at her now he wasn't
sure he was willing to lose the strange sight she brought back into his
life. What was he going to do with her then?

"I see." Her eyes flickered briefly as they darted around the forest. He
could see the wheels in her brain spinning as she tried to formulate a plan
of escape. They both knew it was useless; she wouldn't be able to get
away from him.

"Where is Jericho?"

Her gaze slid back to him. "Wasn't my day to watch him," she
retorted.

Frustration and annoyance built rapidly inside him, he was used to
her defiance, but he didn't like it, and he wasn't going to deal with it after
everything she had done to him. "I'm surprised you're separated at all, but
then I'm sure you've moved on to someone else by now."

Arianna nodded at him, a cynical smile twisted her full mouth. "You
always did like to believe the worst of me," she muttered, but there was
no offense in her gaze, only a fiery rage that turned them a darker, fiercer
shade of blue.

"And you never failed to disappoint."

True wrath twisted her features; her hand trembled on the bow. Then
she straightened her shoulders and rose unhurriedly from her crouched
position. "I'm glad I held up to all of your expectations." Her back foot
twisted in the earth, digging in as she prepared to make her move soon.
"I hope your fiancée does the same."

He was mildly surprised that she knew about that, but then he should have known that his brother wouldn't keep his mouth shut. "Jericho told you."

"Someone had to, don't you think? It certainly wasn't going to be you."

"When?"

"When what?"

"When did he tell you?"

"What difference does that make?" she snapped for the first time looking disconcerted.

He took a step toward her, but she didn't move away, didn't even flinch. He'd had enough of her defiance, enough of her hostility. She should be telling him everything that he demanded to know. She should be begging for her life like she had begged for Max's, but she wasn't, and she wasn't going to. "Do you have no common sense whatsoever?" he inquired, his voice a low growl as he watched her. "No survival instinct?"

"I live in hell every day," she grated through clenched teeth. "A hell that you monsters created for us. The only sense I *have* is for survival, but since you've pretty much admitted that you're here to kill me I see no sense in worrying about anything else right now, do you?"

He took another step toward her. "I'll shoot this, I swear I will," she hissed.

He quirked an eyebrow in amusement at her threat. She would shoot it, but it would do her little good. "Will you now?"

Her hand clenched around the bow. "Your lackey bastards were near here the other day. They raided one of our encampments. I'm sure you already know that though because I'm assuming one of them spotted me somehow. That's how you knew where to start looking for me." She continued to glare at him as she broke off, waiting for him to say something. When he didn't, she continued on. "There were children in those caves!" she snarled. "*Children!*"

"There are laws, and you and your people are breaking them."

Her eyes fairly sparked with wrath, he could sense her rapidly unraveling control. He had always enjoyed baiting her, watching her response, but this was different, this was not the girl that had stayed in his apartment at the palace. No, this girl was stronger, more callous; colder. This girl fairly vibrated with anger and hostility. She looked like a warrior, she *was* a warrior, he realized. She had always been a fighter, but now she was so much more than that.

She was not the girl that had offered him her vein. She was the woman that was going to fire that arrow at any moment.

"Laws," she sneered. "Laws! You're a worse bastard than those monsters that came here to hunt and kill us. You sit in your golden palace and you use us as your food, and your slaves, and you keep us starving and on the run. And yet you judge me, you hypocritical son of a bitch!"

He had pushed her to a breaking point, pushed her control to the edge. The string of the bow twanged as the arrow sliced through the air. He moved rapidly, dodging out of the way of the lethal projectile moments before it slammed into the tree behind him. It would have been a fatal shot if he had still been standing there, that fact was not lost on him. She had shown no mercy, and neither would he.

He lunged at her. He had expected her to run, to try and flee on foot. It would have been pointless, but it was human instinct after all. What he hadn't expected was for her to take to the trees like a monkey. Heaving the bow over her shoulder, she seized hold of a branch, and fluidly hefted herself onto it. She shimmied up the large tree, moving fleetly through the branches. Braith dove at her, nearly catching hold of her pant leg. Her eyes were round when she glanced back at him, but it didn't slow her down as she scurried up the tree.

She leapt onto another limb and sat for a moment before gracefully rising to her feet. Holding onto the trunk, and the branch above her head, she steadied herself. She stared down at him with narrowed eyes, her breathing was rapid. He had no intention of going up there after her, and she couldn't stay up there all day, but it was only a matter of time before someone came looking for her, or came to the river. He had to get her out of the damn tree. And once he did, he was going to throttle her.

She stared at him for a poignant moment, and then she turned and ran. His mouth dropped, he watched in incredulity as she sprinted easily across the thick limb. She didn't hesitate, didn't pause as she dove off the limb, flying out across open ground before she caught hold of a branch from the tree next to it. He was too stunned to move for a moment, he could only watch as she swung herself easily onto the branch, hopped to her feet and sped across the newest limb. He recalled Jericho's words that no one knew the forest like she did, but it appeared that not only did she know the forest, she seemed to have mastered it. He was still gaping after her when she leapt easily into another tree and vanished from view.

It was her disappearance that drove him into action; he rushed through the woods, following her as she leapt and dove and ran through the trees with the agility of a squirrel. He had never seen anyone move like she did, so effortlessly and easily. She was heading deeper into the forest, drawing him farther away from the area she had been walking toward when he found her. She was trying to lead him away from her family, and friends.

She raced down another limb, he watched in dismay and amazement as she leapt out of the tree, except there wasn't another tree to catch hold of this time. She folded in on herself, curling her arms around her legs as she spun through the air. He had no idea what she had in mind until she hit the ground. She landed easily on her feet and bounced swiftly up. She darted through the woods in a zigzagging pattern, easily avoiding any obstacle in her way. It was amazing to watch her, amazing to see her sleek agility, and her profound knowledge of the world around her.

Though he was fascinated by it, and felt that there were still many things she could do, many secrets and abilities that she had hidden, he was tired of being avoided. She was heading toward another large tree, if she got into it they would continue to play this game of cat and mouse. He poured on the speed, rushing after her, unwilling to let this continue. She had just thrown her arms around the tree branch when he caught hold of her. She didn't cry out, didn't scream as she planted her legs against the trunk and shoved off it with all of her might.

He stumbled slightly backward as she lurched sharply against him with the full force of her small weight. He kept hold of the collar of her shirt though, clinging to her as she tried to dart forward, tried to pull free of his hold. She was far more stubborn, wild, and determined to escape than he had thought she would be. He knew she was a spitfire, but she was a lot more volatile than he recalled her being. She flung herself forward; the thin material of her clothing tore within his rigid hold.

She staggered, just as surprised as him to be momentarily free of his grasp. He grabbed at her, wrapping his arms around her waist as he caught hold of her. She cried out in surprise as they tumbled to the ground. Though he didn't care about her, he shifted his weight away from her, trying not to crush her beneath him as they rolled over the ground. She was frantic now, squirming against him, her terror evident as she tried to escape his ironclad grasp.

He was surprised by the brief moment of guilt that tugged at him. He wanted her to pay for her perfidy, but he hadn't meant to terrify her to this extreme. She tried to stagger to her feet, but he kept hold of her waist, pulling her back underneath him as he flipped her over. Her eyes were wild as she thrashed against him, her hair was a straggling mess around her flushed face. She was panting beneath him, her fright palpable as she continued to try and writhe out of his hold.

He seized hold of her hair, his hand wrapped into the thick, wet mess. She pushed at his chest, shoving against him as a whimper escaped her. He didn't know what he was thinking, what he was doing, but instead of burying his teeth in her neck and draining her dry as he had imagined doing for the past couple of months, his lips descended upon her mouth, seizing hold of it. Her hands flattened against his chest, she went still as stone beneath him. He pressed tighter against her, requiring some sort of response, needing something from her, anything.

Needing to break her in some small way, just as she had broken him.

Then, her hands curled into his shirt, her fingers dug against his skin. A small gasp escaped her as her supple lips parted beneath his. She clung to him as her body melted against his. He invaded her, savoring in the taste and feel of her as he melded against her. He forgot everything, all of her deception, all of his hatred and suffering as he held her. It was hard to remember anything when she was so right, and good, in his arms. He had never felt anything as superb as she was, and as long as he held her, he didn't care what happened around them.

It wasn't until he tasted the saltiness of her tears upon his lips that he realized she was crying. It wasn't until he pulled away to wipe the tears from her silken cheeks that he realized he cared for her far more than he had been willing to admit to himself. It wasn't until she rested her forehead against his chest and began to sob heavily that he realized they were both doomed.

~

ARIA WATCHED SILENTLY as the prince threw another log on the fire. She folded her hands before her, clasping them between her legs. Her eyes felt heavy, and raw from crying. Her chest was still sore from the force of the sobs that had wracked her. Despite the heat of the day, she was cold, freezing really. Numb with the shock, and horror, still clinging to her. He turned away from her, the muscles in his broad back flexed as he grabbed another log and tossed it onto the fire.

Aria glanced around the small house he had brought her to. She didn't know why she was here, how he had known about it, but it was a quaint little cottage. He crouched on the floor as he studied her for a moment before rising to make his way to her. "You have to dry off, you're shivering." She didn't tell him that she wasn't shivering because she was still wet and chilled from the river. They both knew that it wasn't the reason. "Arianna?"

She managed a small nod before rising to her feet and moving toward the crackling fire. She settled before it, holding out her numbed hands to the flames. He settled on the arm of the sofa behind her, drawing his long legs up onto the cushions as he watched her. She pulled her hair before her, trying to dry it out and untangle it as she worked through the thick, wet mess.

She didn't know what to say to him, what to do. She didn't know what he wanted from her. She started to shake again; she was trying not to start crying as she recalled the wonderful intensity of his kiss. For one brief moment she had felt whole and alive once more. For one fantastic moment all of the grief of the past few months had vanished beneath his touch, it had all melted beneath the fervor of his mouth against hers. She had been trying to forget how amazing he could make her feel, she had remembered in an instant. And she was fairly certain that she would never be able to forget again.

"When did Jericho tell you about Gwendolyn?"

Her fingers froze in her hair; she turned toward him, admiring the play of light over his striking features. "Gwendolyn?" she asked, baffled by his question, and the name.

"The woman I am supposed to marry."

"Oh." Her fingers slipped from her hair as the numbness returned in full force. She had forgotten about that little detail, that huge, *awful* betrayal. For a moment she couldn't breathe through the pain that constricted her chest, through the knife that stabbed deep into her heart, destroying it. Her fingers clenched in her lap, her nails dug into her palms. If she thought she had any chance of succeeding she might just punch him, but she had already managed to hit him once, in the palace, she didn't think she would get the chance again. "I didn't know that was her name."

His head tilted to the side, he had slipped the dark glasses off, revealing the full beauty of his steel gray eyes, and the bright blue band that encircled his irises. It was so rare when they weren't in place and he relaxed his guard enough to take them off. She could see the faint hint of the scars that marred his striking eyes. Scars that served as a reminder that no matter how remarkable they were, they were flawed and unseeing. "When Arianna?"

She turned sharply away from him, unable to look at him anymore. It hurt too much. "The morning he came to get me."

"*Why* did he tell you?"

She spun angrily back on him, her hands fisted as she fought the urge to punch him. "What difference does that make?" she spat.

He stared silently back at her. "I want to know, that's the difference."

"And I want peace, but we don't always get what we want."

He leaned forward as he glared at her. "I had forgotten how obstinate you are."

She glowered back at him, struggling against the tears that threatened to flow. "Then perhaps you should let me go."

His full mouth curved into a wry smile as he shook his head. "That is not going to happen Arianna. Answer my question."

She shook her head, baffled as to why she was here. Did he just like to torture her by making her rehash the agony she had lived with ever since she had learned of his fiancée? She stared at the fire, watching as it snapped and crackled and shot out sparks. She didn't want to tell him why Jack had told her about his fiancée, she didn't want him to know just how much she had cared about him, then. He had enough power and control over her, without giving him even more.

But she didn't care for him like that, she couldn't care about him like that anymore, she reminded herself. She had been dumb and innocent back then. She would never be either of those things again. Not when it came to him. It didn't matter if he knew why Jack had told her, he had no hold over her anymore.

"Because I didn't want to leave," she finally admitted. Surprise filled his eyes as astonishment rippled through him. "I was foolish enough to think that I would like to stay, with you, no matter what the consequences of that action might have been. Jack simply informed me of what an idiot I was."

"Arianna..."

She launched to her feet, unable to sit still anymore, unable to listen to him. There was a clawing sensation growing inside of her, a desperate urge to be free, a desperate need to escape this whole awful situation. She stepped away from the fire and stopped before the window to stare out at the forest. They were far from the caves, in an area she didn't know as it was close to civilization. It was an area of the woods she didn't travel to, it wasn't safe here. Her fingers pressed against the glass as longing filled her. The sun was out now, her family and friends would be worried about her. They would be looking for her. She had to get back to them; she had to get away from *him*.

"You planned to stay within the palace?"

"It doesn't matter," she whispered. She pressed her forehead briefly to the glass as she inhaled the fresh air seeping through the edges of the pane. "It's the past, it can't be changed. It's over."

She didn't hear him move, but that was not a surprise. It was rare to actually hear his approach. His hands were upon her shoulders, he held her briefly for a moment before deliberately turning her away from the window. When she refused to look at him he gently took hold of her chin and lifted it so that she had to meet his relentless gaze. "I should have told you about her, but I didn't know. I didn't expect..."

"Expect what?" she inquired when he broke off.

He shook his head and bent to place a kiss upon her mouth. "Why were you going to stay?" he inquired, his hands smoothly clasping her face.

She tried to pull away from him, but he held her firmly. He moved closer to her, his chest brushing against hers. His body was a little cooler than hers; the force of his presence was overwhelming. She could barely breathe through the combination of excitement and trepidation pounding through her. She couldn't let herself get carried away here; she couldn't allow herself to hope that this might end differently than it had before. Things could never change between them; they were from completely different worlds. They were from completely different *species* even.

"What difference does it make?" she asked.

He moved even closer, his lips were just centimeters from hers. He was the most irresistible man she'd ever met, even as she tried to fight it, she could feel her body reacting to his, swaying even closer. "Because I *need* to know why you were going to stay Arianna."

"It makes no difference, prince."

"Braith."

"What?"

"I told you once before to call me Braith, not prince."

Aria sighed as she lowered her eyes. Yes, he had told her that before, but ever since she'd fled the palace she had started to refer to him as *the* prince again. It helped her to distance herself from him, something that she desperately had to do in order to survive the heartbreak that had nearly destroyed her. He may like her to stop calling him prince now, but she wasn't sure she could. Doing so would mean allowing him back into her heart.

She didn't think she could survive it a second time.

"Arianna, tell me why you were going to stay."

"No!" her voice was sharper than she had expected. She was ashamed to admit that even she could hear the torment in it. "No! You don't always get what you want. Why can't you just let this be? Just leave *me* be! Why did you come here!? Why did you hunt me down after all this time? How did you even *find* me? I was just beginning to move on and you had to show up and destroy it all again! Destroy *me* again."

She tried to put on a brave front, tried to straighten her shoulders, and raise her chin, but she could feel her lip trembling. It didn't help that sadness filled his features; that a look of loss shimmered in his startling eyes. She almost screamed in frustration. It was all so unfair. She had been trying to move on as she'd attempted to regain some semblance of the life she'd had before he had entered it. But he had shown up again and sharply reminded her of the fact that the only life she truly wanted, but could never have, was a life with him.

"Arianna..."

She tore her gaze away from his, struggling not to cry again. "Please Braith." She was hoping that the use of his name would earn her some reprieve. It didn't.

He kissed her forehead, her nose. Aria shuddered, trying hard not to melt against him, fighting not to give into her desires. But as his lips brushed over hers, she felt herself leaning into him. Felt herself seeking the soothing caress of his mouth and hands. She hated herself for her weakness, but there was something about him, something that she couldn't resist.

His fingers entangled in her hair, he pulled her closer to him as his tongue stroked over her lips. Aria was shaking, trembling, unable to put up any fight against his potent kisses and demanding hands. It was when his hands rubbed over the healing bite on her neck, that she finally came back to herself a little. She tried to pull away from him, but his hand enclosed her shoulder. Ever so gently, he pulled her tattered shirt down a little, revealing the mark upon her. A shiver ran through her as he traced his fingers over it.

She was suddenly flooded with memories of that night, of him upon her, feeding from her, nourishing his body with hers. She had been so enthralled, so unbelievably lost to him, and the joy that had suffused her as he had drained her body of its blood. As he had used her life force to nurture his own. She had never wanted the moment to end, but that was before she knew everything, before she had seen the raid on the caves, before she learned he was promised to another. Another that he probably loved.

Aria pulled her collar away from him, covering the bite back up. There would be no repeat of that night now. She couldn't allow herself to be lost like that again, no matter how badly she craved him. "I loved you," she whispered.

"Excuse me?" he asked in surprise.

"I was going to stay in the palace because I loved you. I told Jack to leave me there, because I didn't care what would happen, what would become of me as long as I was with you. I loved you so much that I thought nothing of my own safety, my own *life*, when it came to you."

"Arianna..."

"And then Jack told me the truth." She continued as if he had never spoken, because if she didn't get this all out now, she never would. If she didn't get it all out, then she would lose herself to him again and it would destroy her this time. "And then my love didn't matter anymore, nothing mattered. *I* didn't even matter. I was so hurt, so mad, so lost and confused and scared. I know you never promised me anything, I know there never could have been anything between us, not in the end, but I never would have allowed it to get that far if I had known the truth. If I had known that you loved someone else, that you were going to *marry* her, I never would have allowed that night to happen. *Never*. You almost destroyed me with your lies and deceit. I will *never* allow that to happen again!"

He stood immobile for a moment, and then he took hold of her chin, holding it loosely between his thumb and index finger. She glared at him, feeling sullen and disagreeable as she folded her arms over her chest. It was childish, she knew that, but she couldn't bring herself to be completely mature at this point. The past two months had been nothing but confusing, frightening, and so unbelievably grueling that she felt she deserved some childish behavior right now.

And now he had reappeared and thrown a giant wrench into all of the hard work it had taken to try and piece herself together again.

"I didn't know Arianna."

"I don't care!" she retorted.

He rubbed his thumb lightly over her bottom lip. "I knew you loved me that night, you told me so, but what I didn't fully understand was how I had come to feel about you."

She struggled to fight against the hope and yearning twisting through her. No matter what he said, this could never be. He would have to leave, and she would have to go back to the woods and the caves. "Don't," she whispered.

"If I had known what was going to happen Arianna, I would have told you about my fiancée myself. I would have left you alone; I would have done anything other than what I did that night. I never meant to hurt you, I swear that. What I feel for you, it's not something I ever expected.

I never thought that it could happen to me. If I had been stronger I would have resisted the offer of your gift until you knew the truth, but that night was a complete surprise to me also."

She stared wordlessly up at him, her mouth parted in distress. "Braith..."

"I don't love my fiancée Arianna. In fact, I dislike her intensely. It's an arranged marriage, her family is very powerful. It's not something that either of us asked for."

Aria was silent as she pondered his words. "That doesn't change anything Braith," she whispered. "You will still go back, and you will marry her, and I will... Well I suppose I will either end up being recaptured, killed, or perhaps even one day I will end up married to Max, or some other rebel. Though it's unlikely I will live long enough for that to happen."

His eyebrows drew together sharply as he moved closer to her, pushing her against the window. Aria stared at him in surprise, taken aback by his blistering anger. "To Max?" he snarled.

Aria frowned at him, she was trying not be intimidated by him, but she was completely baffled by his sudden change. "Yes, I guess, maybe... Oh, I don't know," she breathed. "I have no intention of bringing children into this awful world but he's a good man, he's safe, and he cares for me. Perhaps he even loves me. That should be enough, shouldn't it?"

He was staring at her as if she had just sprouted another head. "You will *not* be with Max."

She blinked in surprise at the growled command; then her pride rose back up. "You're not my father, you can't tell me what I can and cannot do!" she snapped.

His hands were on either side of her, pressed against the window as he leaned ever closer. "You're right I'm not your father, but I am a part of you, and as that part I am telling you that you will *not* be with Max."

She frowned at him, confused by his response. "Part of me? I don't understand."

"My blood flows in your veins Arianna; it's how I found you. It is how I will *always* be able to find you."

Her mouth dropped open, her mind spun. She recalled their last night together, when he had taken her blood. After, she had drifted in and out of confusing consciousness. She had dreamt that he'd held her gently as he gave her something sweet and delicious to drink. Disgust curdled through her at the realization that the sweet drink had been his blood. At the same time longing blossomed like a spring flower as she recalled the tenderness of that night.

"I don't..." she shook her head, trying to clear her thoughts, trying to clear the fog that was clinging to her. "No, it was a dream. Wasn't it?"

The tension melted from his body, his hands were upon her shoulders again as he stroked her neck. "No, Arianna, it was not a dream. It was my fault. I was so hungry..."

"You hadn't been feeding well, because of me. To protect me!" she recalled on a gasp.

"Yes. They couldn't know that I wasn't feeding from you. But I took too much Arianna, you were just so delicious. I took far more than I had anticipated, and the only way to keep you alive was to give you some of my blood. I linked us forever by doing so."

Tears burned her eyes; she looked away from him, staring at the wall over his shoulder. He had also told her he loved her that night, it had all been foggy, hazy, but now that she knew that it wasn't a dream, she *knew* that he had said that as well. He had told her he loved her, and she had left him the next day.

"That's why Jack asked me if I had shared your blood," she whispered.

His hands clasped hold of her face; he turned her back to him. There was a ferociousness in his eyes that staggered her. "Jericho asked you that?" he demanded.

Aria swallowed heavily as she nodded. "Yes, when he came for me, when he saw the blood still on me, he asked me if I had shared your blood. But I thought that it had been a dream, I was *certain* of it once he told me you were engaged." She thought his teeth might crack if he clenched his jaw any tighter. "Would he have left me there if I had answered differently?"

He shook his head; his dark hair fell around his face, highlighting the hard planes of it. "I don't know what he would have done Arianna. If anything, these recent events have made me realize that I don't know my little brother at all."

Aria clasped hold of his hands, holding them tenderly against her face. She closed her eyes, savoring in his gentle touch, savoring in the strength of him. Yes, he did have a fiancée. Yes, she couldn't expect much, if anything, from him. However, he had loved her, he had told her so. He had not merely been using her, playing with her in order to cause her even more anguish when he turned on her.

"You said you loved me," she whispered.

He pulled her closer, enfolding her in his arms as his body melded to hers. "Yes."

She wanted to cry again, for everything they'd almost had, for everything that they *had* lost. For everything that they *would* lose, and could *never* have. But it was impossible to feel sad when he was holding her. It was impossible to hurt when he was kissing her forehead soothingly, nuzzling her ear, touching her with such reverence and awe. She let herself drift into him, let herself get lost in him. These past months had been so awful, but his touch eased all of the rawness and sorrow that had been clinging to her. His touch made everything better; it was the salve to the ragged lesion that had been festering since their separation. For just this moment, in this time, she needed to feel better.

She needed to feel *him*.

# CHAPTER FIVE

ARIA WOKE LEISURELY, her eyes were heavy and sleep clung to her. It was the first time she had slept without being plagued by nightmares since she'd left the palace. The first time she didn't wake up in pain, the first time she could awaken and actually breathe easily again. Her gaze instantly fell upon Braith; he was standing by the window, staring out at the darkening night. Aria lay quietly, savoring in this blessed moment of peace, but all too soon realization crashed back over her.

She bolted upright, distress rolling through her as she stared at the night sky. The day was gone. Braith turned toward her, his eyes troubled as he studied her. "My father is going to be so worried, my family; my friends." Though the words were going to kill her to say, she said them anyway. "I have to go Braith."

He turned back to the night, before looking at her again. "It's late Arianna."

"I know, but..."

"Tonight, just tonight."

She stared at him wistfully, her mouth parted as her heart hammered in excitement. She so badly wanted to stay with him for this night, and for every night after this. She couldn't have those nights, but she could have this one. Guilt briefly tugged at her as she thought of her family and friends, but it was only one night. It was the only night she would have for the rest of her life. It was wrong, she was being selfish, but for once she didn't care.

"Ok," she said in a hushed voice.

His mouth curved in amusement, his head tilted to the side. "I expected more of an argument."

She grinned back at him as her fingers played with the cushion of the couch. "I'm not always difficult."

"Could have fooled me. Come." He held his hand out to her as he walked over to her. She slipped her hand into his and smiled shyly at him.

He led her down a darkened hall, flicking on light switches as he moved. The mouth watering scent of food hit her before they even reached the kitchen. Her mouth parted, her eyes widened in surprise as she stepped into the room. Food was set up on the counters, cheeses, breads, fruits, and meats were stacked neatly upon two plates. She glanced around, wondering who had done this, but there was no one else within the small house. Her gaze fell upon Braith, who was watching her in amusement.

"You did this."

"I'm not completely helpless," he replied flippantly. She couldn't help but grin back at him. It was one of the sweetest things anyone had ever done for her. She didn't stop to think about what that said of her life, it wasn't worth it. She was good at getting by with very little. "Come on, you're hungry."

She didn't ask him how he knew that, her stomach was rumbling loudly, and repeatedly. She settled onto a stool at the counter while he heaped food onto her plate. She cocked an eyebrow at him, amused by the amount of food he was piling on for her. "I'm not starving," she told him.

"You've lost weight again," he replied as he slid the plate before her.

Aria shrugged; there was no help for it in the forest. They didn't have enough to eat, and they worked endlessly. "Thank you." He sat across from her as he folded his arms across his chest. Aria studied him for a moment, feeling self conscious as he watched her eat. "What is this place?" she inquired.

"It belonged to my mother's family, it was their summer getaway."

"Really?" Aria glanced over the large, airy kitchen. "It's very nice. Will they come looking for you here?"

"Jericho and I were the only ones that ever came here, except for some cleaners once a week that replenish the food just in case we bring a human with us."

"Why did the two of you come here?"

Braith shrugged as he sat back and folded his arms over his chest. "To hunt, to get away. To be alone for awhile."

"To get away from what?"

"From many things," he replied evasively. "Eat Arianna."

She picked up a piece of apple and began to chew on it. She barely tasted its sweetness in her mouth as she thought over his words. "*Will* they come looking for you here?"

"No. I doubt my father even remembers where this place is, and Caleb is busy. They won't even notice I'm gone."

"What about Jack? Will he come here looking for me?"

Confusion filtered through his eyes before realization dawned. "I forget you call him Jack."

Aria smiled as she leaned toward him. "It's what we know him as. He certainly isn't a prince to us."

He grinned back at her and poked her nose before settling back in his seat. "I suppose he isn't. But no, Jericho will not come here. I doubt he will even think of it."

Aria nodded, relieved to know that they wouldn't be disturbed tonight. She settled in, a large weight lifting off of her as she eagerly dug into the delicious food. They talked easily, exchanging stories. She told him what it was like to grow up within the forest. She told him about her father, and her brothers Daniel and William. She told him of things she'd been too frightened to tell him about before, when he hadn't known that her father was the leader of the rebels. She didn't know much about her mother, she'd been killed when she and William were young. Her father didn't talk about her very often, it was too painful for him, but when he did talk of her Aria listened intently, eager to learn anything she could about the woman that she had never really known.

Though she told him many things, she didn't tell him any details about where they were located, and exactly how they operated everyday. She believed she could trust him, but there was still too much between them to even think about giving him any of those details, and he didn't ask.

Though Braith listened to her, he didn't say much about his life. His mother was also dead. He didn't speak of his father much, and when he did, Aria got the feeling that he didn't like him, and that they didn't get along. He barely mentioned Caleb, or his sisters, he spoke a little more of Jericho, and though she caught the underlying tension in his voice, she also caught the only hint of fondness she'd heard toward any of his family when it came to his youngest brother.

She enjoyed listening to him talk, and thought she could do so forever. Even though she knew that was impossible, she decided to pretend that just for tonight, they could have forever. It was amazing to be his equal for a change, and not his slave. The moon rose high in the sky, and was beginning its downward descent when he stood. "You must be tired."

She was tired, but she wasn't going to go to sleep. She wanted to savor every moment of this night. She could sleep tomorrow when he was gone, and she was alone again. "I'm ok."

He slipped his hand into hers and pulled her against him. His hand wrapped around the back of her head as he cradled her against him. She held him, simply relishing in the feel of his firm body against hers, committing to memory the feel of being in his arms again. She gasped, amazement racing through her when he bent and scooped her easily into his arms. She stared down at him in delirious wonder as her fingers stroked the nape of his neck. His eyes, intense and burning, never left hers as he easily strode from the room.

He navigated the dark hallways with ease until he stopped at a door that he thrust open. He didn't bother with the light switch as he strode over and placed her tenderly upon the bed. Aria watched him as he moved around, drawing the curtains shut and blocking out the fading moon. Her heart hammered with excitement, her mouth was dry as uncertainty claimed her. She didn't know what was going to happen, what he expected, or what she was even willing to give to him. She would like to pretend that they had forever, but they didn't. Yet, it was Braith. Even if she never saw him again, she knew she would never love anyone the way she loved him. This was more than likely their last night together, if she was never going to see him again, didn't she want to give him everything she could?

He was as silent as a ghost as he came back to her and slid onto the bed beside her. He pulled her against him, kissing her softly. All doubts and concerns vanished; she wasn't going to think about it, not now. And he made it so very easy to forget everything, except for him. His hands caressed over her face, her hair, as he pressed her into the bed. His eyes were bright in the dim illumination of the room as his hands smoothly clasped each side of her face.

"You are beautiful."

She had never thought she was, but she felt beautiful when she was with him. She felt as if she were the only woman in the world, and in some ways, to him, she was. She was the first woman he had seen in years. She lowered her lashes as tears burned her eyes, she didn't want to think about anything else, but she couldn't help it. This was it. This was all she would have of him.

"Arianna?"

She lifted her eyes to him and forced a smile. "I'm fine Braith, I'm ok."

He kissed her nose, pulling her against his side as he rolled off of her. "There are some other things I have to tell you Arianna. I'm not looking to upset you but I don't want you to be surprised by anything you hear about me."

She frowned as she lifted her head to look at him. He looked troubled, his eyes were distant, haunted. "What is it?" she asked.

His fingers slid through her hair as he ran it through his grasp. "Before you, I never had a blood slave."

"I know."

"After you..." his voice trailed off for a moment, his fingers tightened briefly in her hair. "There were many."

Aria stared at him in surprise, and then the sharp stab of betrayal seared through her with the intensity of a lightening bolt. It took all she had to continue to breathe through it. She had thought that she was special. No, she *was* special to him. She couldn't start thinking like that, couldn't let herself start to doubt that fact. It would ruin this small bit of bliss they had managed to find together. She was special to him, he *did* care about her. She just had to keep believing that it was true. He wouldn't be here if it wasn't. "Why?" she choked out.

His gaze was relentless upon hers; there was a defensive, almost defiant air about him. "I was trying to forget."

"Forget what?"

"You."

She knew how that felt, the driving need not to think about anything, not to feel anything anymore, if only for just a brief moment in time. "Did it work?"

"That's why I'm here." She managed to smile feebly at him, but she couldn't shake her lingering hurt. "I never gave them my blood Arianna; I've never done that with anyone else."

She managed a small nod, trying not to show how upset she was. She knew that she was failing. "It's ok."

"Arianna, I thought... I don't know what I thought. That's the problem I was determined not to think."

"I know Braith, I understand how you felt, how it hurt to think, to breathe even. I know because I didn't want to think or feel anymore either. I don't like it, but I understand. It's... It's what you had to do."

She could barely speak by the time she was done, tears clogged her throat, but she couldn't find it within herself to be angry right now. She hadn't been there for him, she'd thought that he had lied to her, and he'd thought that she'd betrayed him. She couldn't be enraged when he was looking at her with such a vulnerable, needy expression. He may not have given them his blood, but she was sure that he had done other things with them, things that they hadn't even done together.

Aria quickly shut the thought down. It had no place here, this was *their* night, he was being honest, and she could not fault him for that. He'd bared himself to her, even though it hadn't been necessary for him to do so; she was already in his bed. She didn't approve of what he had done, she would never condone it, but she wasn't going to let it ruin this night, she couldn't.

"And what did you do to stop from thinking?" he asked faintly though she heard the tension in his voice.

He had buried himself in women, and blood. She had buried herself in the woods, in the wild, in the solitude. "Went fishing."

He lifted an eyebrow in amusement. "You went fishing?"

"Yes, I'd go to the lake almost every day and go fishing. It was so peaceful; I could lose myself in the nature and serenity of it. Even when Max..."

"Max?" the name was almost barked at her.

She frowned at him. She had taken his disturbing news relatively well; he owed her the same respect. "Yes, Max. He *is* my friend. He was also a blood slave, though his experience was far worse than mine. He needed the solitude, the peace, the company of someone who understood at least a little of what he had gone through. He would join me, and we would just silently sit together."

"I think Max would like to be more than a friend," his voice was low, gravelly as he grated the words at her.

"Braith..." She didn't know what to say, what to do. She started to deny it, she knew it would only irritate him, but he was being honest, so she should be too. "Yes, he does. And at one time I had a big crush on Max. He was older, my brother's best friend, and my first kiss." Braith's hand tensed on the back of her head. "But even before we were blood slaves, even before I met *you*, I had decided that it could never be between us."

His struggle to keep himself calm was evident in the tight press of his mouth. "Why not?"

Aria shrugged. "My life isn't one that I would wish on anyone else, especially not a child. It's too brutal."

He was silent as he studied her before pulling her down to him. His lips were warm against hers, smooth, and soothing. His hand cradled the back of her head. She lost herself to him again, forgetting everything and everyone. The effect he had over her was amazing and absolute.

He kissed her lips, and then her nose, before pulling back from her. "It will all be ok," he whispered. "Everything will work out."

She managed a wry smile as she nodded. They both knew that it wouldn't be ok, but here, tonight, in his arms, she could believe anything. She fell into his kiss, losing herself to the touch and feel of him. He was amazing, everything she had always coveted, and could never have. He rolled her over as his mouth moved leisurely over her neck. He pulled her shirt down to reveal her shoulders. He stilled upon the bite mark, his lips hovered over it as she felt the sharp press of his fangs against her flesh.

"It's ok," she breathed, her fingers curling into his thick hair. "It's ok Braith."

He didn't hesitate, but bit down, reopening the bite marks and causing her blood to spurt once more. Aria arched against him, but the sting was sharp and fleeting. Then she felt the familiar tug of her blood into his body. But unlike the first time, he was not half starved and almost out of his mind with hunger. He was far more serene, and far more caring as he moved over her. She clung to his rigid arms, tears streaming down her face as she savored in the wondrous joy of the moment. She never wanted it to end, never wanted to part from him as his pleasure slipped into her and his happiness filled her.

He pulled away from her, holding her as he wiped the tears from her cheeks. "Don't cry Arianna."

She couldn't stifle the tears or the emotions streaming from her. She ran her hands over his beloved face, trying to memorize every detail of him before they were separated again, this time for good. He slightly pulled away from her and bit deep into his wrist. She couldn't tear her gaze away as blood flowed from him. Unlike the last time, she would remember this exchange.

She felt she should be repulsed by the idea of drinking his blood. The vampires were her enemies after all, they always had been, but she didn't feel revulsion as he held his wrist out to her. The need in his eyes was glaringly obvious, and she wasn't going to turn him down. She would never hurt him in such a way. She watched him as she brought his wrist to her mouth. His eyes sparked with desire and love.

His blood was sweet as it flowed into her, powerful as it seeped into her cells. He kissed her forehead, his nose rubbed briefly against hers as he nuzzled her neck. "I love you too Arianna," he breathed, his mouth hot against her ear. His words only caused more tears to flow.

∼

ARIA WOKE to the smell of something delicious cooking. She smiled contentedly, stretching out upon the comfortable bed as her stomach rumbled in eager anticipation. She didn't know what he was cooking for her now, but it smelled fantastic. Upon crawling out of bed, she discovered the bathroom, and the shower. Drawn by the lure of hot water, she was unable to resist climbing into the shower. She discovered the robe on the back of the bathroom door after forcefully removing herself from the dwindling heat.

The robe smelled of him, which made it even more irresistible to slip on. The velvety material felt fantastic against her bare skin. She hesitated a moment, self conscious about going bare beneath the robe, but she wasn't ready to put her clothes back on. They weren't filthy, but they most certainly weren't as clean as the robe, and she was going to enjoy her brief reprieve for a little while longer. She didn't think Braith would mind.

She slipped from the room, following her nose as she padded silently down the hall. "Something smells amazing, and I've decided the shower is the best invention ever."

She turned the corner, holding the knot on the front of her robe as Braith came into view. He was standing in the kitchen doorway, his back to her. She frowned, uncertain as to what he was doing there. His head turned toward her, his gaze was dark and stormy as he spotted her. She hesitated, confused by his obvious distress. They'd been fine when they'd fallen asleep, better than fine even. She'd never felt so content and happy in her life, never felt so close to someone else.

And now it seemed as if the sight of her was enough to send him into a rage. Aria began to shake; her hands trembled on the knot of the robe. What was going on?

His eyes narrowed severely, and then his hand slammed into the doorway with enough force to splinter the wood. Aria jumped as the wood cracked loudly and bits of it scattered to the floor. Her heart leapt in surprise, but she still didn't feel any fear, not of him anyway. He wouldn't harm her she knew that, she just didn't understand what was wrong with him right now.

He turned away from her; his back ramrod straight, his muscles quivering beneath the thin fabric of his shirt. Aria looked away from his rigid back, her eyes widened and her mouth dropped when she spotted Jack on the other side of the room. He was standing by the outside door, staring at her. There was surprise in his features, but there was also confusion and a resonating sadness that shook her.

It was then that she realized their wonderful world of bliss had been forever shattered once more. "Aria," Jack greeted.

She itched to reach out to Braith, but her hand remained frozen on her robe. She didn't know what to say or what to do. She was practically naked, standing in their family house, her hair wet and straggling. She knew what it all looked like, and she didn't care. What she cared about was the fact that Jack had found them. That he had come here to ruin their brief time together, *again*. Irritation shot through her, they'd had so little time together as it was, especially as equals, and now it was over.

She glared at him, her hands fisting at her sides. Jack quirked an eyebrow as he studied her questioningly. "I'm assuming you didn't force her here," he stated flatly.

"No," Aria responded, when Braith didn't.

Jack stared at her for a moment before turning his attention to his brother. "What are you doing Braith?" Jack muttered.

Braith's body remained rigid but the arm that slammed into the wall shook as his knuckles turned white. Aria knew that it was more than just Jack being here that was shaking him, but also the fact that their time together was over. They both knew Jack was here to take her back, and there was nothing that either of them could do to stop it. She had to go back to her world, just as Braith had to return to his.

"That's none of your business," Braith grumbled.

Jack's eyes flashed with annoyance. "It *is* my business. She's a young girl, you have no right..."

"I'm not a child!" Aria interrupted sharply. "And you are not my father, or my brother, Jack."

Jack's gaze was remorseless. "No, your father and brothers would have come in here looking to kill; they would have been appalled to find you like this." Aria recoiled from his harsh words, she felt as if she'd been slapped by him.

"Don't," Braith snarled. "Don't talk to her like that."

"You have no idea what you have gotten yourself messed up with here Aria," Jack continued as if Braith had never spoken. "And yes, you are a *child*. Especially when compared to us. You are a small blink in our lifespan Aria. You should know better Braith, I thought *better* of you than to do this with a young girl, a *human* girl no less! What are you doing!?"

Braith bristled at the reprimand, the muscles in his back rippled. "Like I said before, that's none of your business."

Jack's upper lip curled as his eye did some twitching motion that would have been amusing if this wasn't so awful. "How did you even find her? What are you even *doing* outside of the palace?" Neither Braith nor Aria answered him. Jack glanced rapidly between them, then his shoulders slumped and his gaze landed upon her. "You lied to me."

Aria shook her head. "I didn't lie to you."

"Then what do you call it!?" he exploded. "I asked you if he had shared his blood with you! You told me no!"

"I'm not going to tell you again to watch how you talk to her!" Braith bellowed.

Aria grasped hold of his arm as she sensed his rapidly unraveling control; he was nearing a volatile snapping point. She wasn't going to let them fight, not only were they brothers, but she had a feeling that they would destroy this house, and each other, if they did. She wasn't about to let that happen because of her.

"It's ok Braith." He relaxed somewhat, but a tremor remained in his muscles, and she wasn't fooled into thinking that he wouldn't attack at a moment's notice. "I didn't remember Jack; I thought it was a dream. I didn't lie to you on purpose, it was..." She didn't know what it was, she couldn't explain it. "I'm sorry Jack."

"Don't apologize to him," Braith told her.

"You put us all in jeopardy," Jack scolded.

Aria stepped closer to Braith, needing his touch to ease her raw nerves. He glanced back at her, his eyes softening as he took her in. She stared up at him for a moment, trying to calm her racing heart. He finally released his hold on the wall to pull her against him, and move her behind him a little to try to block her from Jack's scrutiny.

Aria rested her forehead against Braith's chest as she took a deep breath, trying to calm her raw, savaged nerves. Braith wrapped his hand around the back of her head, holding her for a prolonged moment as he bent his head to hers. "Why don't you go get dressed Arianna," he whispered in her ear.

She shook her head; her gaze darted back toward Jack. "No, I'm not leaving you."

"It will be fine," he assured her. "I'd much prefer you in clothes though, ok?"

She felt vulnerable at the moment and would love clothes, but she was unwilling to leave the two of them alone together. "No Braith."

He grunted impatiently, she could sense his frustration with her, but she was not leaving here if there was even the smallest chance that they were going to attack each other. "Go Aria," Jack told her.

"Jack, we may be friends, but you have to stop treating me like a child." Jack's brows lifted in surprise. "Both of you," she added, turning her attention back to Braith. "I'm not as old as you, but I've seen and experienced a lot. So no, I am not leaving here until I am certain that you will not kill each other."

Braith's jaw clenched in annoyance, Jack's mouth quirked in sardonic amusement. "Well apparently she disobeys everyone, even the mighty future *king*," Jack drawled. Braith shot him a ferocious look. "Are you going to be his queen Aria? Oh, but you could never be the queen there's already somebody set up to produce heirs for him. Will you be the mistress then, the kept woman?"

She flinched from the sharp reminder that she couldn't be his queen; that she never would be. Her fingers dug tighter into Braith, she labored to breathe through the anguish constricting her chest. "That's enough!" Braith bellowed. "You say one more word and I'll tear your tongue out Jericho, do you understand me!?"

"One more word of the truth?" Jack demanded.

Aria held on to Braith as he tried to pull away, tried to lunge at his brother. "Stop Braith, please. Just stop, both of you, stop!" Braith tried to shake her free, but she somehow managed to insert herself in between the two of them. "*Stop!*"

Aria was breathing heavily, she was terrified she was about to witness two brothers kill each other. She didn't realize that the sleeve of her robe had fallen down to expose her shoulder, until Braith grabbed hold of her. Pulling her back, he yanked the sleeve up to cover her skin, and the dark mark upon it. It was too late though, Jack hadn't missed the fresh bite upon her. He stared at her covered shoulder, before finally lifting his startled gaze to hers.

"I told you, I am here willingly," Aria informed him.

# CHAPTER SIX

BRAITH CLASPED the robe around her, surprised to realize that she was not wearing anything underneath. He had at least expected the thin night-gown he had set out for her, but perhaps she hadn't noticed it, or she had simply chosen not to put it on. Either way, she was not wearing clothes. He didn't know if he was more excited by this prospect, or infuriated by it. Though, if his brother hadn't been standing there, Braith knew what the resounding answer to that question would have been.

Arianna seemed oblivious to his surprise over this new development as she continued to glare defiantly at Jack. Braith's gaze turned back to his brother. "I came here willingly, and I know that there is no future for us Jack. You don't have to continuously remind me of something that I am painfully aware of. I wanted this. I *needed* this."

Though her voice was strong, Braith could see the tears in her eyes. "Aria," Jack said morosely, looking lost and dumbfounded.

Her fingers curled around Braith's arms. "I know everything," she told him. "I know it all, and I accept it for what it is Jack."

"Do you know about the blood slaves?" Jack demanded. "The many he has kept in the past few months? Do you know what he has done to them, *with* them Aria? You are not special!"

Though Braith still thought of him as his brother, he was beginning to realize more and more that this man before them was not the Jericho he had known, but was in fact more the Jack that Arianna knew him as. This was not the same brother that had left the palace six years ago, it was not the same Jericho that Braith had grown up with and been close to. This man was a stranger, one that seemed determined to tear Arianna away from him. He didn't think it was because Jericho had romantic feelings for her, but in fact had come to think of her as a sister, or a good friend. One that he was trying to protect, unfortunately Jericho was trying to protect her from *him*. Jericho also seemed determined to hurt her in his attempt to get her away from him.

Jericho just didn't realize that he was trying to keep her safe from someone that would die to make sure that she stayed that way also. Braith knew that the man across from him was not Jericho, but was in fact the man that he had rebuilt himself into. He was now this man called Jack and Arianna knew him far better than Braith did.

Arianna glanced up at him, biting on her bottom lip as her eyes swam with tears. Anger surged through Braith; she had been jerked around enough. He couldn't stand the fact that she had to experience even more of it. He cradled her face in his hands, savoring in the feel of her silken skin. "I know about them too," she said quietly.

Braith rested his forehead against hers; taking a small moment to enjoy the peace and splendor she brought to his hectic world. The last thing he'd ever wanted was to reveal to her what a monster he'd been these past couple of months, but he was now immensely glad he'd done it before Jack had. "You are special," he assured her.

"Shit," Jack whispered. He pulled a chair out from the table and limply slid into it. "What have you done Braith? What have the *two* of you done?"

Braith kissed her lingeringly before pulling back. "I put some clothes out for you; they're on the chest in my room. Please go get dressed Arianna." She glanced at Jack, her forehead furrowing in consternation. "We'll be fine," he assured her.

She paused for a moment more before finally nodding her consent. He watched as she hastily moved down the hall, warily glancing back at them before slipping around the corner and disappearing from view.

Braith turned back to his brother; he folded his arms firmly over his chest as he studied him. Jack didn't know that Braith could see the incredulous look on his face, didn't know that he was watching his brother's every move.

"What is this between you Braith?" he inquired.

"I don't know," he answered honestly.

Jack frowned at him, his hands curled upon the table. "She may think that she can handle this, but she can't. She's strong Braith, she's seen a lot, but she's also very innocent to the ways of the world. You didn't see her after I took her away from there. You don't know her the way that I know her..."

"What is *that* supposed to mean?" Braith demanded.

Jack sighed as he leaned forward in his chair and clasped his hands before him on the table. "I've been in the woods for *six years* Braith. I've seen firsthand what these people suffer through, what *our* kind has forced them to suffer through. I've known Aria for over four years now, she's proud, she's wild, and she has one of the kindest hearts I've ever known. She's been broken ever since I pulled her out of that palace, ever since I took her from *you*. She may think she can handle this, she may even feel that she is prepared for it, but compared to us she *is* just a child and it's obvious that she's in love with you."

Braith shifted as he glanced behind him to see if she was coming back yet. He was bristling, resentful of his brother's words, and the fact that Jack seemed to think he knew so much more about her. "She is more than a child," he grated.

"She is *seventeen* years old! You are to be king; you are to be married..."

"I don't need you constantly reminding me, or her, of that fact!" Braith snarled. "I was not lucky enough to be born the middle, or the youngest son. I was not lucky enough to get the chance to leave that place, and all of my responsibilities, behind. I was not lucky enough to escape father's brutality!"

Jack pondered his words before finally answering. "I know that Braith, probably more than anyone, it was why I left in the first place. Though, at first I'd thought to win father's favor by doing something daring and perilous. I aimed to earn his respect, and I was going to make him realize that I was more than just a punching bag. Once I was free though, I realized just what a monster he is by living amongst the people that he has mistreated even worse than us. Aria's family, and Aria herself, are the biggest contributors to this realization and I care for them. You're my brother, I love you, but I'll never return there and we no longer share the same goals. These are my people now, I will protect them."

"And you think that I won't protect her?"

There was a hopeless air around Jack as he studied Braith. "I think you will try, but there is only so much you can do. You hate father as much as I, but you have always been big on responsibility and duty. You will not turn your back on that. That is why I didn't tell you that I was going to take her. I knew you would stop me simply because it would weigh heavily on your conscience to be involved with such treason."

"You have been gone for awhile Jack; you don't have a clue as to what you're talking about," Braith growled.

Jack's hands sprawled on top of the table as he half rose from the chair. "And why is that?" he demanded. Braith glanced back down the hall. Arianna was still out of sight, but she would return soon. He turned back to his brother, Jack had become a man in the time he had been gone, but Braith still saw the little boy in him. "You're to be married Braith, you are to take over for father. That is your world, this is not..."

"*She* is my world," Braith interrupted sharply.

Jack's gaze slid past him but Braith's hand had extended toward Arianna before she arrived at his side. She took hold of his hand, squeezing it between both of hers as she held it before her. Jack studied the two of them before sliding back into his chair.

"Dear God Braith, this is a mess," he breathed. "Your father is worried about you Aria."

"I'm sorry for that." Jack ran his hands through his shaggy hair, nodding as he played with the fork Braith had placed on the table. "How did you know I was here?"

"I didn't. I knew *Braith* might be here."

Arianna glanced up at him, frowning in consternation. "I didn't think he would look for me," Braith admitted. "I didn't think he would expect the two of us to be together, and even if he did, I didn't think he would come here."

"I see," she murmured.

"I only *hoped* that you had brought her here, and not returned her to the palace. I only *hoped* that it was not someone else that had taken her," Jack explained further.

"Now you trust me with her?" Braith grated.

Jack quirked an eyebrow as he tilted his head. "No matter what I've heard about you recently, I still believed that father had not succeeded in destroying all of your humanity as he has with Caleb. I knew you would be infuriated that I took her from you, I half expected you might try to find her again just to soothe your pride, but I didn't think you would punish her for something that I had done."

Braith continued to glare at his brother, infuriated with him. It was the faint rumbling of her stomach that finally pulled his attention away from his sibling. "You should get something to eat Arianna."

"Braith..."

"I can hear your stomach rumbling." Her face flared red as she ducked her head. "Come on."

He led her forward, pulling out the chair for her to sit. He watched his brother suspiciously as he unhurriedly pushed the chair in. Jack was frowning, his forehead creased as he studied them. Arianna stared back at him, her gaze distrustful and resigned. Braith made her a plate of food and slipped it in front of her.

She hesitated for a moment, but eventually her hunger won out. She eagerly dug into the eggs. "You can see!" Jack blurted in astonishment.

Arianna froze with the fork halfway to her mouth, her gaze darted to Braith. She didn't even breathe as she anxiously watched him. Braith rested his hand reassuringly on her shoulder. "I can," he confirmed.

"What? When? *How?*"

Braith shrugged, he settled into the seat beside Arianna. "Eat," he encouraged. She took a few more bites, but he could tell that her appetite had vanished beneath her apprehension.

"*How* Braith?" Jack pressed.

He turned back to his brother, keeping his hand on Arianna's thigh. Jack may have taken her from him, but he was one of the few people in the world that Braith trusted with Arianna. "I don't know," he answered honestly.

"But your vision is back? You can see again?" he asked excitedly. For a moment his irritation and disbelief was gone as pure joy for Braith blazed forth. Braith had never complained about being blind, had taken it in relatively easy stride, but he had hated it. Jack had known this, and sympathized with him because of it.

"Sometimes I can, yes." Jack frowned in confusion. Arianna was unmoving, he could hear the forceful beat of her heart, sense the anxiety that ran through her. He had told her not to tell anyone about his ability to see only when around her. Jack wouldn't harm her though, of that Braith was certain. He ran his hand over her thick hair, savoring in its silken feel as he tried to ease her tension.

"And other times?"

"I am still blind."

Jack was completely confused, but Braith felt no need to elaborate more. He felt he could trust his brother with her safety, but Jack had taken her from him, he had betrayed him, and in all honesty Braith liked keeping him in the dark and confused. It was a minute amount of payback, but at least it was something. Arianna remained silent, her mouth compressed in a taut line as she watched them. She picked her fork back up and began to eat again.

"Well that's strange," Jack muttered.

"I suppose it is," Braith agreed.

"When did this start?"

"A little while ago."

Arianna continued to pick at her meal until she finally pushed the plate away. "I should get back soon. I've already caused my family enough worry."

She didn't look at either of them as she uttered the words. He could hear the sorrow in her voice, the strain it had caused her to say those words. He leaned closer to her, inhaling her sweet scent as he briefly nuzzled her hair. She finally turned toward him, her eyes morose, but there was an air of resignation and steely resolve to her.

"Arianna..."

She smiled thinly at him as she stroked his cheek. "Thank you for bringing me here. Thank you for giving me last night."

He grasped hold of her hand, hating to see her like this, hating the distance he felt her putting between them. "Not yet Arianna."

She smiled sadly at him as she turned her cheek into his hand. "Yes, it's easier to just do it now. Jack will take me back. It will be ok."

There was a forlorn look on her face as she squeezed his hand and rose. His chest constricted, panic tore through him. He couldn't lose her again, he simply couldn't. The chair skittered back as he leapt to his feet. "Arianna..."

"Its fine Braith, we'll *both* be fine." Though she said the words, her heart was beating loudly. "We'll be fine," she said again.

He pulled her firmly against him. He could stay here; he could become like Jack and hide in these woods. He could stay with her, help with the rebel cause. Make sure that she was safe. They could both be happy. But even as the thought crossed his mind, he knew that he couldn't. His father hadn't destroyed the forest in search of Jack, but if Braith were to leave, and his father was to discover why, he would destroy everyone, and everything, in order to find him and punish him. If he ever found Arianna...

Braith couldn't finish the thought, it was too awful. What his father would do to her in order to punish Braith would be horrendous, atrocious. He couldn't put her in such a position, couldn't risk her life in such a way. She buried her head against his chest as she embraced him whole heartedly.

She reluctantly pulled away, her head bowed. He grasped hold of her chin, tilting her head up to kiss her. She melded against him, a low sigh escaped her. He barely registered the sound of the door opening and closing as he lost himself to the astonishing feel of her. It was awhile before he roused himself from the sweet taste of her mouth.

Unblinkingly she stared up at him and then a small smile curved her mouth. "I am going to miss that."

He ran his finger over her swollen lips. "I can come back," he said impulsively. He had never planned to come back, it was too much of a risk to her, but faced with the prospect of never seeing her again, the words had popped out of his mouth. "I *will* come back."

Tears slipped down her cheeks. "Braith, you're getting married."

He shook his head, his thoughts turning dark. The last thing he cared to think about was his upcoming wedding, and the bitch he was marrying. Especially not when he was holding the woman he desired to spend forever with. "I'll come back Arianna, as soon as I can. I will be back. I *will* find you."

"Won't it be risky for you?"

"I'll find a way," he vowed, stroking her face.

She smiled tremulously. He could tell that she wanted to argue with him, wanted to tell him no, but neither of them were strong enough to walk away. Not right now anyway. He kissed her again, before taking hold of her hand and leading her to the door.

Jack was standing near the forest, his back to the house. He turned at the sound of the door opening. Arianna's hand clutched in his, a tremor worked its way through her. "The blood slaves Braith, do you..."

"There will be no more Arianna." She was trying to believe him but her eyes were still doubtful. He knew that she could forgive him for these past months, she hated what he had done, but she had understood what had driven him to it. She wouldn't forgive him, or understand him, if he continued on such a path. There could be nothing between them then; he would not be the man that she loved if he continued to mistreat her people, and he wasn't willing to lose her again by stooping so low once more. Sensing her uncertainty, he bent over her as his hand stroked over her cheek. "I swear Aria there will be no more blood slaves."

She smiled feebly as she managed a small nod. He kissed her soothingly, his attention turning away as Jack came toward them, his eyes weary and sad. "Make sure that she stays safe until I can come back," Braith grated.

"You're coming back?" Jack's mouth dropped as he stared at the two of them.

Braith glared at him. "Yes."

# CHAPTER SEVEN

ARIA GLANCED up at Max as he stepped closer to the map laid out in the middle of the cavern. His eyes were dark and intense as he stared down at it, his eyebrows drawn sharply together. William stood beside him, his arms crossed over his chest as he bit thoughtfully on his bottom lip. Aria's father was talking in hushed tones, his dark head bent over the map as Daniel traced a line through it with a stick.

Daniel was the only one of them that had inherited their mother's fair coloring. His hair was wheat colored; his fair skin speckled with freckles that made him appear far younger than his twenty one years. His eyes were the same bright blue as Aria and William's though. Aria sat back on her heels, her legs were cramping up, but she couldn't move away from the map. She was far too fascinated, and horrified, by it.

She focused her attention on Jack. He was standing off to the side, his arms folded over his chest as he stared at the back wall. Ever so slowly, his gaze came down to hers. It took all she had not to leap to her feet, grab hold of his arm, and drag him from the cavern and demand to know what he was thinking.

Aria glanced back down at the map, swallowing heavily as Daniel poked the spot where the palace was. She'd always had the rudimentary knowledge necessary to read a map, but Braith had taught her how to read so much more. She didn't share this revelation with the people surrounding her; she didn't think they would appreciate it much, and no matter what she said or did, they would continue to believe that she had been manipulated by Braith. She was tired of trying to convince them they were wrong, it was wearing on her, beating her down, making her everyday struggle to just survive even more tiresome.

"Is this how you remember it?"

Aria didn't realize her father was talking to her until she noticed that they were all staring questioningly at her. She swallowed heavily, trying to wet her suddenly parched throat. "I guess; I didn't really pay much attention. I didn't get out much either," she finished on a whisper.

Though it wasn't memories of being kept as a blood slave that made her voice tremble, her father seemed to think it was. He gave her a sympathetic look before resting his hand on her shoulder. He had been treating her like she was fragile ever since she'd returned. She was becoming frustrated with it.

"Max?"

Max was standing off to the side, his arms folded over his chest as he stared at the far wall. His jaw was locked, his forehead furrowed. She hadn't been abused, but he had, and now her father was talking about going back in there as if it were the simplest, easiest thing in the world. About *all* of them going back in there. "From what I recall, yes."

Aria's heart hammered and flipped, she could barely breathe through the terror constricting her chest. "You can't do this," she whispered. "It's slaughter to go in there, we can't."

Her father patted her shoulder again before rising to his feet. He knew that this was reckless; he knew that it was crazy, but he seemed determined on doing it anyway. And she knew that it was because of her, because he believed that she had been abused during her time with Braith. It didn't matter how often she told him that she hadn't been; he was convinced she was lying.

He moved away from the map as William and Daniel leaned closer to it. "We'll send a small scouting team in first, have them canvas the area. They will be able to discover the weakest areas, and the best places in which to establish our soldiers. We will have to take the palace swiftly."

"Dad," she whispered, clutching her hands before her. Her legs were shaking, her head was spinning. "The last time someone tried to take the palace it was a massacre."

He wasn't paying attention to her though as he moved away. Dread was thrumming through her. She couldn't allow this to happen, she couldn't allow people to die because her father sought revenge for things that had never even occurred. At least not to *her*.

But they had happened to other people, and they were continuing to happen right now.

However, the rebels had made an attempt to take the palace when she was a child, and they had been decimated. In retaliation for the rebel's defiance, the king had sent out thousands of troops that had razed, burned, and slaughtered their way through villages and forests. It was how her father had become the leader. He'd been elected after the last one had been brutally murdered, and his body hung within the largest village as an example of what would be done to others who tried to attack the palace.

"We will have to be smarter about it this time, go about it in a more methodical way."

"I would like to go in," William volunteered.

Aria's mouth dropped, she spun on her brother, her twin, her other half. "No William," she breathed. "You cannot go in there."

"Yes, I can."

"No! Your coloring, you're too similar to me. They'll know you. Tell him Jack. Tell him!" She was practically begging as she turned frantically to Braith's brother. "Tell him about Caleb, and what kind of a monster he is. Tell him what Caleb would do to him if he discovered him in there! Tell him he is a *fool*! That they *all* are!"

"Arianna, enough," her father said sharply.

"Who is Caleb?" Daniel inquired.

"My brother," Jack answered.

"The middle one," Max elaborated.

"I thought you were held by the oldest brother," Daniel said.

Aria was shaking as she tried to regain control of herself. Acting crazed and wild wouldn't get them to listen to her. It would do none of them any good if she was a raving lunatic. She must remain calm and collected if she was going to talk them out of this crazy suicide mission.

"I was," she said. "Braith is a good man..."

"He's not a man," Max interrupted.

Aria glanced at him, hating the betrayal and abhorrence that radiated from him as his scathing gaze landed upon her. They would hate her, they would all hate her if they knew the truth, but at the moment she didn't care. "My oldest brother believes in duty and honor. He highly values them both," Jack told them.

"Including holding young women hostage and using them," her father interjected sharply.

"Braith was kind to me," she said for the thousandth time, but none of them listened to her.

"Caleb is not like Braith, or me," Jack continued, his glance at Aria was sympathetic but tough. "Caleb is like our father, cruel, twisted; vengeful. If he discovers that you are Aria's brother he will torture you in ways that you can't even begin to imagine. Your hair color alone might be enough for him to take his revenge on you."

"But your older brother wouldn't?" William inquired the scorn in his voice more than apparent.

Aria could feel Jack's unrelenting gaze upon her. She didn't know what to say, what to do. If they found out that she had just been with Braith, that she intended to see him again, they would go ballistic. They would think she had lost her mind, that her time as a blood slave had twisted her. They wouldn't stop to think that she was with him because she truly *did* love him; they would assume that she had lost her mind, and they would lock her away. She would never see Braith again, and they would all run off half cocked, determined to avenge her for absolutely no reason other than bullheaded male stubbornness.

"No, he wouldn't," Jack admitted.

Aria was too ashamed to look at him anymore. She was running around behind her family's back, and yet she was sitting through this horrendous meeting discussing how to invade the palace. Something that could get Braith seriously hurt, if not killed. Something that could get members of her family killed.

She had spent her entire life fighting against the vampires, trying to destroy them, and now she found herself frantic to do anything to stop this.

"Well isn't the future king special," Max drawled.

"He is," Aria insisted.

Max's lip curled in disgust, her family stared at her as if she had sprouted another head. "Ok William can't go in then, but I can," Daniel said.

"Daniel," Aria moaned, she dropped her head into her hands as her mind spun. She had to think of something, anything that would stop this. She turned back to Jack, but he was leaning against the wall again, his arms folded over his chest. "You don't know what you're doing."

"Yes, I do."

Aria could barely breathe through the lump in her throat, could barely see through the tears burning her eyes. She had to stop this, she didn't know how, didn't know what to do, but she knew that she had to stop this. She didn't know when Braith would be back, she didn't know if she should even tell him what they had in mind. She'd be betraying her own family if she did. She'd be betraying her own kind.

But if she remained silent and something happened to Braith, or someone in her family...

She shut the thought down. She couldn't live with herself if something happened and she could have stopped it. Her legs gave out; she slid to the ground, her mind spinning as they continued with the plans that were slowly tearing her in two.

ARIA KNEW that she shouldn't do it, but she couldn't stop herself from slipping through the woods, back to the lake. It had become her favorite place over the past couple of months, and now that she needed it the most, she was not supposed to go near it. But after the events of the past few hours she didn't give a damn what she was, or was not, supposed to do. Not anymore.

She slipped through the forest, sticking to the trees, remaining hidden amongst their thick foliage as she darted from limb to limb. She kept an eye out for any threat. She knew the forest better than anyone, knew the signs of danger. She could read the animals as well as she could move through the trees. They remained alert, and active, the birds continued to sing, the squirrels hopped eagerly in out of the branches. They barely noticed Aria's presence amongst them.

Reaching the lake, she sat amongst the limbs of a tree as she surveyed the area around her. The lake was pristine, clear. There wasn't even a ripple disturbing the glass surface. She folded her hands beneath her, resting her head upon them as she sprawled out on the limb, content to lie amongst the branches and watch the activity within and around the lake and find solace in the beautiful vista before her.

She didn't realize she had drifted off until she tried to roll over and nearly fell from the tree. She awoke with a start, sitting up on the branch in surprise. She hadn't even been tired, but the events of the day had beaten her down, and taken more of a toll on her than she'd realized. Her gaze turned to the sky, judging by the movement of the sun she'd been asleep for a couple of hours.

She would have to go back soon, but before she returned she was going to take a quick swim. She kicked her shoes off, letting them drop to the forest floor before standing. She ran to the end of the limb and dove into the lake. She stayed beneath the water, swimming out a ways before popping back to the surface. The water was refreshing and cleansing after the awful events of the day.

She swam for a brief period before heading back. Stopping a few feet away from the shore, she treaded water. Jack was leaning against the tree with her shoes dangling from his fingertips as he watched her. Aria frowned at him as she pushed the hair from her eyes and swam forward.

"You have to stop taking off like that."

"I can take care of myself." She grabbed her shoes from his hand, but didn't put them on. "What are you doing here?"

"Looking for you."

"Did my father send you?"

"No, they're still making plans. What are you going to do Aria?"

"What do you mean?"

"Are you going to tell him?"

Aria couldn't meet his gaze. The water had managed to calm her for a brief moment, but now she was back in the harsh reality of her life. "Are you?" she whispered.

"He is my brother, but I chose my loyalties when I took you from that palace. I cannot go back on that now."

"You would allow him to be killed?"

He shifted in distress but his eyes were sad and accepting. "He would allow the same thing to happen to me, if the roles were reversed. He would hate it as much as I do, but we are on separate sides of this war. There is nothing that we can do about that. Now *you* have to choose a side Aria."

She shook her head, hating the fact that she had the urge to cry again. "How can I choose a side Jack? It's not so simple. If I choose him then I forfeit my life, there would be nowhere for me to go after that. If I choose my family than I am giving up the only man that has ever made me feel this way, the only person I have ever been in love with."

She followed as he made his way through the forest. "I didn't say it was going to be an easy choice, it wasn't for me either. But it is one that you are going to have to make, and soon."

"I don't know when he'll be back," she whispered.

"He won't be away for long..."

"You don't know that."

Jack stopped abruptly and turned to face her in the dwindling daylight. The strong resemblance he bore to his brother tugged at her heart. He watched her with the same intensity that his brother always did, studied her with the same confusion that she had often seen on Braith's face. It seemed that neither of them knew exactly what to make of her. But then, she didn't know exactly what to make of *them* either.

She'd thought Braith a cruel, monstrous bastard, and now she was in love with him. She'd thought Jack a human, her friend and rebel companion, but it turned out that he was actually a vampire, and a member of the royal family. She'd been kept in the dark about Jack's identity, because they all thought her too weak to be able to handle the truth. In truth, she was far stronger than any of them knew. There was far more to her than they had ever imagined. The only one that seemed to understand, and accept the true depth of her strength, was Braith. He was the only one that didn't try to coddle her, didn't try to shelter her from the harsh realities of both of their existences. He was the only one that *knew* she was strong enough to handle it.

And if there was one thing she was becoming very tired of, it was being coddled.

"I *do* know it, and by the time he comes back you are going to have to make your choice."

"What if I choose wrong?"

He glanced over at her, his eyebrows lifted as he studied her. "I don't think you *have* a right choice here Aria."

"You're right. Are you going to tell my family about this?"

Jack shook his head as he started walking again. "No. Braith is not a threat to them. Even if you choose them, he will not go after them, that's not who he is. If you don't choose him he would not purposely hurt you in such a way. No matter how much it will hurt him if he loses you."

She grasped hold of Jack's arm, pulling him to a stop beside her. "I do love him," she said forcefully.

He managed a small smile, his hand enclosed hers. "I know that Aria. And though it is baffling to me, I know that he loves you."

She frowned at him, not at all liking his comment. "Thanks."

He grinned at her and squeezed her hand before releasing her. "As the future king, Braith always kept a part of himself distant, aloof. It would always be his job to uphold his duties and responsibilities, and to Braith those responsibilities always came first. I didn't think he would ever be capable of loving someone; he kept himself too separated for that. You may be the first thing he has ever chosen over his obligations. The first sign of disloyalty he's ever exhibited toward our father."

Aria was silent for a moment, and then she resumed her pace at his side. "But he hasn't chosen me."

"He's chosen you more than I've ever seen him choose anything else. He came here for you, didn't he?"

Aria shook her head. She watched her bare feet as they moved through the forest, avoiding any obstacle that may pop up. She didn't tell him that she was fairly certain that Braith had originally come here to kill her, or at least make her pay severely for her disobedience. "I choose your side over my family."

Aria brushed aside her damp hair as she glanced up at Jack. "Why?"

she questioned, still not completely understanding why he had taken their side.

"Because once I was here, I realized that I had been on the wrong side. There's no reason for anyone to be living like this, there is no reason for the cruelty that has been bestowed upon the humans. Not anymore."

"It sounds like you picture a world where we can all happily coexist."

He shrugged. "I'm not delusional. I don't believe it will be easy, but I do think things could have been different, maybe even still could."

"Perhaps." Though, she didn't hold out much hope for that.

"You are going to have to stop taking off on your own though. Not even Braith can help you if you get caught again, and what Caleb would do to you..." His voice trailed off, his eyes were distant as he stared at the woods around them.

Aria didn't even want to *imagine* what Caleb would do to her. He'd unnerved her from the moment she'd met him. There was something wrong with Caleb, something sadistic and cruel. He would take great pleasure in making her scream, in making her beg for mercy. Caleb would delight in making her suffer.

Aria shuddered, she tried to shut the thought down, but it wouldn't stop. "Ok?"

She swallowed heavily as she nodded. She hated to be monitored, but Jack was right. "Ok," she agreed.

He slid his arm though hers, pulling her against his side. "I think of you like a sister."

She managed a weak smile as she leaned against his side. "An annoying one?"

"Yes. You are also going to have to do something about Max."

"Max?" she asked in confusion.

"He's in love with you." Aria frowned, her hand tightened on Jack's arm. Jack was right, she had to make it clear to Max that there would never be anything between them. She hadn't been fair to him lately. Telling him no, while still leaning on him to help get her through the past few months. Guilt and self hatred twisted through her stomach, Max was going to be hurt again because of her. She knew now though, that even if she never saw Braith again, he would always own her heart. There could never be anything between her and Max. "And he's not very stable right now."

"The woman that held him, she was awful to him in there, wasn't she?"

Jack seemed hesitant to confirm her words but he'd never sugarcoated anything for her before. "She was, and Max is convinced that it was the same with you."

"I've told him it wasn't."

"It's easier for him to think of us as monsters. If I hadn't pulled the two of you out of there, he would hate me too. He still doesn't trust me."

Aria frowned as she glanced up at him. "Do you think he would do anything to hurt you?"

Jack shrugged. "He might try, but not for awhile, not until things are more established. He knows that I'm needed right now, but after..."

Aria stared at him in surprise. "And you're not angry about this?"

He glanced down at her. "What was done to him in there was something awful Aria. We will never know the extent of the cruelty he experienced, of the abuse that he took. No one comes out of that completely normal. I understand his resentment and his hatred. But if he tries to kill me, I will not hold back."

Aria swallowed heavily, she hated the awful situation they were stuck in, hated the fact that she would have to choose between Braith and her family; hated the fact that she was becoming increasingly worried and fearful of Max.

# CHAPTER EIGHT

"Do you ever do what you're told?"

Aria didn't bother to look up from the berries she was collecting. "Not usually."

"You know you're supposed to stay close."

She glanced up at Max as he stopped at her side. His shadow fell across her, blocking out the sun. "I'm close."

"Within eyesight Aria," he said brusquely.

She dropped the berries into her bucket as she fought to maintain her patience. She hated being ordered about, hated his high handed demeanor, but most of all she hated the fact that he felt he had any say over what she did, or didn't, do. She wasn't far from the caves, everyone knew where she had gone and had been fine with it. Except, apparently, Max. "I have my bow," she reminded him.

"That will do a lot of good against a group of marauding vampires."

Aria rolled her eyes as she wiped her hands and rose to her feet. "I'm perfectly capable of taking care of myself," she reminded him.

"So capable that you were caught already."

Aria heaved an impatient sigh; she grabbed hold of her bow as she tried to ignore the tugging waves of guilt crashing through her. She didn't think she would ever be able to forgive herself for what had been done to Max, but she couldn't continue to live under the weight of that guilt. She also couldn't allow him to continue thinking there was any hope for them. Even if she gave Braith up, she wouldn't choose Max.

"I'm fine Max."

"I understand you require solitude Aria, I do, but you have to understand that I'm only concerned about your safety."

"I know." She was just agreeing with him in the hope that he would back off. Aria jumped in surprise when he seized hold of her chin. She frowned fiercely at him, trying to keep her temper.

"I know you feel that this raid is a bad idea, I know you think that he treated you kindly in there, but..."

"Max I can only tell you so many times that I *was* treated kindly in there. I know you had an awful time, I *know* that, but you have to believe me when I tell you that I didn't. This raid isn't just a bad idea, it's an awful, *horrible* idea. I know you want revenge, but risking innocent lives isn't the way to get it."

He glared at her. Jack thought that Max was in love with her, but at the moment she felt that he might actually hate her more. "Max," she whispered.

His shaggy blond hair fell across his forehead as he shook his head. "You don't know what you're talking about Aria. What they did to you in there, it's confused you."

Aria wanted to argue with him further, but it was useless, and something else had caught her attention. She tilted her head, her eyes narrowing as all of her senses focused upon the forest. Aria glanced around the shadowed woods, panic hammered through her as she realized the birds had stopped singing and the squirrels no longer ran through the trees.

"One day you'll realize..."

Aria slipped her hand over Max's mouth, and placed her finger over her lips as she motioned for him to be silent. He frowned at her, but she'd stopped paying attention to him. She could read the woods better than a book, and right now they were telling her that something wasn't right, that there was a threat out there. She just didn't know what direction it was coming from, didn't know which way to flee. She tilted her head back, glancing into the high branches of the tree.

She pointed up as she took her hand away from his mouth. Moving silently, Aria grasped hold of the lowest limb and easily scooted her way through the branches. Max was not as quick as she was, but he followed her. Aria climbed higher, burying herself within the thick foliage. She searched the forest but still saw no cause for the odd silence that had descended over it.

She bent down to grasp hold of Max's hand to help pull him onto her branch. His skin was paler and he looked as if he were about to throw up. He had always hated heights, but they didn't have many options right now. He opened his mouth to speak but she shook her head vigorously at him. She still couldn't find the danger hidden within the shadows.

And then she saw them. They had come from behind the tree, and were underneath it before she knew what had happened. She plastered herself against the trunk of the tree, grasping hold of it as Max pressed against her. Aria was shaking, if they looked up...

If they looked up, she and Max were dead. Max couldn't move through the trees like she did, and even she couldn't outmaneuver a group of vampires forever. They would catch her eventually. Her heart was thumping so loudly that she was certain they would hear it, certain that they would look up and spot them within the foliage of the tree. Aria's breath caught in her throat, she could barely breathe as Caleb appeared beneath them, moving leisurely behind the six soldiers before him. His head moved constantly as he searched the woods. The excitement strumming through his body was nearly palpable.

Her legs were trembling so bad that she could barely stand anymore. Max was frozen before her, his lean body hard as rock as he pressed against her. If Caleb was here then only bad things could follow.

Aria froze, her mouth dropped as Braith stepped into view behind his brother. Her heart leapt, flipping wildly as she took in his magnificent form. Longing erupted through her, she almost called out to him, almost flung herself from the tree, and into his arms. And if it hadn't been for Caleb mere feet before him, she probably would have.

It had been a week since she had last seen him; a tortuous week that had been filled with uncertainty, trepidation, and a desperate yearning that was shaking her thoroughly now. She had gone two months without him, had spent two months trying to forget him, but this past week had been far more grueling. There was no hatred and anger within her to fall back on now when she craved his touch. Her fingers twitched, she almost cried for the unfairness of this whole situation. She remained frozen instead, motionless with the dread that had locked her muscles into place.

Braith stopped, his head turned from side to side and then tilted back. She knew the minute that his shaded eyes locked onto them. Max took a small step closer to her. She could barely breathe as she was squished against the trunk of the tree. Though his jaw clenched and a muscle jumped in his cheek, Braith showed no other sign that he'd seen them.

He turned away from them, moving onward through the forest as the small troop disappeared. Max relaxed against her as he breathed a sigh of relief. "Good thing your former master is blind."

Aria was fighting against tears and the need to scream in frustration. She ached to tell Max that Braith had seen them, that he *knew* they were there, and that he would keep them safe. She thought it might help him to understand that Braith wasn't bad, that he was in fact a very good man, and that he loved her. She thought it might help Max to understand that not all vampires were evil, but she couldn't bring the words to leave her throat. She had promised Braith that she wouldn't tell anyone his secret, and she meant to uphold that promise, even if it meant continuing to alienate her friend.

"We have to warn the others," Aria whispered.

Max nodded, he moved away from her as he began to gingerly make his way from the tree. Aria hesitated as she searched for any sign of Braith, and the others. They had moved on though. She descended rapidly, dropping silently to the ground beside Max. They moved swiftly through the forest toward the campsite they had left behind.

"What are they doing here?"

Aria shook her head helplessly. How was she supposed to know what they were doing here? "I don't know Jack."

"Did Braith tell you about this?"

"No," she retorted in exasperation. "I would have prepared people if he had. I sure wouldn't have been hanging out in a tree with *Max* if he had! In case you didn't realize it, they don't exactly like each other."

The look he shot her was more than a little irritated. His eyes were cold and thoughtful, his face dark. "He may not have known that Caleb planned to come here."

"Of course he didn't know! He wouldn't have left me out here unprepared if he had known."

"Aria..."

"He wouldn't have Jack," she insisted, infuriated that Jack would even think such a thing. Infuriated that she was also thinking it, even though she knew it was wrong.

"He knew we were in that tree Jack. If he was here to harm us, or to recapture us, he would have turned us in. I couldn't have escaped them all, and I wouldn't have left Max behind."

"He might not have seen you. He said himself that his vision comes and goes; we have no idea of knowing how good it is when he does have it."

"I *know* he saw me," Aria insisted unwilling to discuss how she knew this.

Jack paced away before rapidly coming back. He stopped before her. "I don't know what this bond is between the two of you, I don't know what to say about it or what it means, but I do know that it has put us all in peril. Especially if Caleb has come with him."

Aria glared at him. "Did you stop to think that maybe Braith is here because *Caleb* decided to come here first? Did you ever think that he is here to offer what protection, or help, he can?" she demanded. "You say you and Braith were close, and that you were good friends, yet you have no faith in him. You have no idea what kind of a man he truly is!"

"And you do?" he demanded.

Aria stared defiantly back at him. "Yes."

He cursed loudly before anxiously pacing away again. Aria was unwilling to follow him as he headed toward the dark, cavernous area of the caves. The last thing she wanted was to be trapped within the caves again, but that was where everyone had already retreated with the hope that they would stay safe. He turned back to her, but she remained unmoving just feet from the cave.

"Aria!" he hissed.

It was a challenge to keep breathing through the constriction in her chest. She had never truly liked the caves, but now she found herself terrified by the prospect of going back in there. Her skin was clammy, she was shaking. She found she would almost prefer to be in the hands of Caleb than back in there, trapped amongst the cold rock.

She took a small step back as Jack came toward her, frowning in puzzlement. "Aria?"

"I can't," she whispered. "I can't go back in there."

He stared at her in disbelief. "Aria you *must*," he insisted.

She shook her head again, taking another step back. Her heart was thrumming, her whole body was shaking. His gaze raked over her, then turned back to the caves. "I'll be fine in the trees," she told him.

"Like hell," he retorted.

"I'll be safer in the trees than in there! I can move through the trees faster than I can through the caves."

"You can't stay out here Aria; we can't take the risk of you being captured again."

He was coming at her before she even had time to blink. A scream welled in her throat, but his hand was over her mouth as he lifted her up and forcefully carried her toward the caves. Aria thrashed against him, trying to break free of his ironclad hold. Then he entered the cave and she was consumed with the urge to be free of the confining space, and stale air. She couldn't breathe, she couldn't think as her head began to spin rapidly. She went limp against him, struggling to inhale through her nose as he carried her deeper into the earth.

They were half a mile down before he finally released her. Aria fell to her knees, trying to catch her breath, struggling to control the rapid beat of her heart as a scream rose in her throat. She didn't know what was wrong with her, what was happening to her, but she couldn't control the wild, frantic sway of her body. She tried to choke back the scream, but she couldn't keep it bottled within her anymore.

It ripped free of her, echoing loudly through the cavern, bouncing off of the rock walls in an endless wave that sharply pierced through the air.

# CHAPTER NINE

BRAITH FROZE IN MID STEP, his foot hung in the air as his head turned to the side. He tuned out the normal sounds of the forest, filtering through the noise as he strained to hear what had caught his attention. He was certain that it had been a scream, certain that it had been *Aria's* scream. His foot dropped upon the forest floor, crackling the leaves and sticks beneath his boot. The men with him stopped walking as they turned back to him.

"What is it?" Caleb demanded.

Braith shook his head. His brother hadn't heard the scream, neither had the others. He didn't know if it was because they weren't as attuned to Aria as he was, or if it was the fact that his hearing was more acute due to his blindness. At his side, Keegan bristled, turning to survey the area of the forest Braith was certain that scream had come from. "It's nothing," he replied.

Though it was far more than nothing; that scream had been echoing and terrified. And it had come from the only person that he cared about. "I have to go."

"Wait what!?" Caleb stammered.

Panic seized hold of him; it clawed at his chest, and tore through his insides. He had to get away from his brother, and he had to find her. He had seen her in the tree with that *boy* and if he had done anything to hurt her Braith was going to destroy him. He moved rapidly through the trees, blurring as he raced across the forest. Though he could not see his surroundings, he could sense the obstacles in his way and easily dodged them. Keegan was unable to keep up with him, but Braith knew when the wolf broke off and retreated deeper into the woods.

The others tried to keep up with him, but he was faster and stronger than them, and he lost them easily amongst the forest. He jumped on top of a boulder, racing up the side of it before leaping off the top. Trees began to blur into focus, wavering on the outskirts of his vision. He could smell her blood, taste it in his mouth again. He was getting closer to her.

Thirst spurted through him, his veins burned with the intense need to feed. He hadn't fed since he'd left her a week ago. He'd returned to the palace, but no one appealed to him anymore, not even the willing humans he'd fed from before. In fact, he was surprised to realize that the mere thought of feeding from anyone else was repulsive to him. It was *her* blood he required and until he could feed from her again, no one else would do.

Then, for some strange reason, Caleb had insisted upon going on one of the hunting parties. Braith had known that he'd have to go with him, he couldn't take any chances that Caleb might accidently find her without him being there. The thought was horrifying to him. He'd come with Caleb to make sure that such a thing didn't happen, and it nearly had earlier, and might still happen if Caleb was somehow able to track him.

He skidded on a patch of leaves as he came to an abrupt halt outside of a tapered crevice between the rocks. He would have missed it if he hadn't been tracking her. He slipped into the hole, barely fitting in between the boulders surrounding it. His eyes adjusted to the blackness, picking up the small bits of illumination within the enshrouding dark. Her sweet scent became stronger; her fright was nearly palpable within the confines of the cave.

Braith moved through the winding, snug turns, keeping his senses attuned to other presences as he moved through the cave. He had to get to her, but he knew he had to proceed with caution. He had just placed himself right into the heart of the lion's den, he was certain of that. He was surrounded by rocks, walls, and his enemies. He felt like a rat trapped within a maze as he stalked her scent. He couldn't believe that they lived down here. That *Arianna* lived down here.

She hated to be confined, hated being trapped anywhere. She was everything that the woods were; open, wild, and free. It was confounding to him that she could be beneath the earth within these stale confines.

Her scent enveloped him as he turned another corner, he could hear voices as they carried through the tunnels in the cave. He stopped, his head tilting to the side as he picked up three male voices. One of them was Jack, but the other two he didn't recognize. He crept closer, straining to hear the words.

"What happened?" one of the strange voices demanded.

"I don't know," Jack answered. "But we have to get her out of here. We have to move, now."

Braith bristled, he assumed the *her* was Arianna as her scent was exceptionally strong here, and his vision was nearly perfect again. He hesitated within the shadows. "Be careful with her Jack! Watch her head!" the other strange voice commanded. "Damn it, give her to me."

"I've got her Max."

"Give her to me!" Max snapped back.

"Just give her to him Jack; you're going to have to keep your hands free if they come in here."

Braith's hands fisted, a haze of red shaded his vision. It was bad enough that his brother was touching her, but he definitely didn't like that *boy* holding her. There was a muted rustling, and then Arianna made a low, disgruntled sound. "Put me down!" she ordered. "Max, put me down!"

"Aria..."

"Let go of me! Let go of me!"

"Aria..."

There was the sound of scuffling and then she groaned loudly. "Stop, please." Her voice was a low moan of anguish. And it was more than he could take; he was going to kill someone.

He stepped around the corner, bloodlust surging through him as he took in the spectacle before him. Jack was standing toward the back of the small opening, his face like stone, and his jaw clenched. Arianna was struggling against the boy holding her, Max, as she tried to tug her hand free of his restraining grasp.

"Stop Max, let her go." The other boy stepped forward, he reached for Arianna as her struggles to break free became more frantic. "Aria, you have to calm down. Please."

"Let me go!" she snapped as her breath came in rapid pants. Braith had only ever seen her like this once before, and it had been when she'd thought that Max's life was in jeopardy. Then, she had been terrified for her friend. Now the terror was all her own, something he had thought was impossible until this moment.

"Let her go."

Their heads snapped toward him, their mouths dropped in surprise. "Braith," Jack whispered in dismay.

A small cry escaped Arianna; she was finally able to tug her hand free of Max's as he relaxed his grip. She ran at him and flung herself into his arms. He lifted her, cradling her against his chest as she buried herself against him. Wrapping his hand around the back of her head, he threaded his fingers through her silken hair as he briefly savored the feel of her in his arms again. She pressed closer to him as she shook within his grasp.

"Shh Arianna, shh," he soothed. "What happened?"

"Braith what are you doing here?" Jack demanded.

He bowed his head briefly to hers, pressing his mouth against her silky hair as he eagerly inhaled her sweet scent. She was the best thing that he'd ever felt, the best thing he'd ever held. Jack moved away from the wall, the astonishment of Braith's sudden appearance was beginning to wear off of the other two. He didn't miss the stake that appeared within Max's grasp. Jack grabbed hold of Max's arm, holding him back as his Max leveled him with a killing glare.

"You know what I'm doing here," he said to his brother. He adjusted his grasp on Arianna in order to keep his body in between her, and the growing hostility of the men across from him. He grasped hold of her face, smoothly pulling her away from his chest. Her shoulders were still heaving but she seemed to have regained some control of herself. "Are you ok?"

She managed a nod, her bright eyes were questioning as she studied him. "It's not safe for you here," she whispered.

"I know." He looked back at the others, his eyes resting upon the redhead who was gaping at the two of them in shock. His gaze deliberately turned toward Arianna before coming back to Braith. Max looked like he was about to snap, anger radiated from every inch of him as he glared furiously at the two of them. "Did they hurt you?" he growled. He didn't care if they were her friends and family, he was spoiling for a good fight.

"You shouldn't be here," she whispered fervently, her hands clutching at him as her eyes became frantic. "Braith..."

"It's ok Arianna," he told her. "I'll be fine."

"She's right Braith, you have to leave," Jack insisted. "Where's Caleb?"

"Elsewhere."

"Braith..."

"He doesn't know where I am," he interrupted sharply.

"But he could find you, and by doing so, find us."

"He could also find you." Jack became silent; his eyes were hooded as he gazed at Arianna. She was still shaking, but her tremors were less severe now. "Did they hurt you?" he demanded again. He would hate to do it, but he would kill Jack if he had harmed her in anyway.

She shook her head, biting on her lip as dread shimmered in her eyes. "I don't like it down here."

Of course she hated it in here. He had known that she would. "I'll take you out then."

"No," Jack inserted sharply as the other two men took a step forward. "She has to stay with us, and she needs to be somewhere safe. It is *not* safe above ground right now."

"I'll be safe in the trees," she told him.

"No Aria, absolutely not. We have to meet up with your father."

"No, no, no. I am *not* going deeper; you can't keep forcing me to!"

Braith ran his hands over her hair, trying to calm her, but failing as she continued to shake like a leaf against him. "He forced you down here?" Braith demanded.

"Braith..."

"Back off Jack or I'll snap your neck if you take one more step toward her, if you touch her one more time!"

"No," Arianna interjected. "You can't fight, not here, not now. Please."

Braith's hands tensed on her shoulders, he was trying to keep her behind him, but she kept insisting on trying to get in front of him. "Who do you think you are?" Max demanded.

"Don't push me!" Braith snarled at him, fighting the rising tides of hostility surging through him. They had forced her down here, forced her into this place that was obviously terrifying to her. Jack pulled Max back a step, but the other man remained immobile as he watched them intently.

"Don't push *you*!" Max snapped back as he fought against Jack's restraining hand. "You're lucky I don't kill you!"

"You could try, but you will not succeed."

Rage flashed across Max's face. Jack pushed him back as he tried to lunge forward. Max strained against him, but Jack was successful in keeping the smaller man pinned against the cave wall. "Stop it!" Arianna commanded loudly. "Stop!"

She was still shaking, but he could also sense growing exasperation beneath her terror. Max's gaze raked scathingly over her, glaring at her from head to toe. Braith bristled beside her, pulling her further back from the infuriated boy. He didn't trust Max. He knew that Max would kill him in a heartbeat, but he was beginning to worry that he might also injure Arianna in his rage and hatred.

The other boy shot Max a dark look as he placed himself in between them. "I'll go up with her."

"No William," Arianna told him as she shook back her dark hair. Braith took note of the striking similarities between Arianna and this boy. He remembered Arianna telling him about her twin, remembered Jack talking about the similar hair color; it was more than obvious that this was him. "It's safer for you to stay here."

"I'm not letting you go up there alone." His sapphire eyes were intense as they turned toward Braith. He considered Braith, his gaze not trusting, but not hate filled either. Not like Max's.

"I won't be alone," she reminded him.

"Aria..."

"I'll be ok William, really."

William remained hesitant. "No Aria that is not going to happen."

"I can keep *her* safe, I can't promise that for you," Braith told him.

William nodded. "That's fine."

"No," Jack said forcefully. "I can't risk the two of you being captured. That is too much leverage over your father should something go wrong."

"I will keep her safe," Braith said in a low, deadly tone. "And you don't have an option here Jack; I'm taking her out of here no matter what you think."

Arianna's fingers curled in his shirt, she pressed closer and her forehead rested briefly upon his chest. "You're being foolish Braith. I know you don't like seeing her upset, but would you rather see her dead? Be logical about this, she is safest down here!" Jack protested.

"I am being logical about this, and I am telling you what is going to happen. I will keep her safe. When you return above ground, you know where we'll be."

"You can't take her to mother's house. Caleb will go there."

"I'm not taking her to the summer house."

Jack was silent for a moment, and then realization dawned in his eyes. His mouth dropped, his fingers twitched at his sides. For a moment, his grip on Max eased. "You know what that means if you go there Braith."

"I do. Find us when you are able to." He turned his attention back to William. "You must stay here. She will be fine, but I can't protect you both."

"No." William was shaking his head forcefully. "Absolutely not. She may trust you, but I don't."

"You have to," Jack told him. "You can't go with them William."

"You can't seriously be considering letting them leave here! Of letting this *monster* take her back!" Max exploded his face was florid. "Have you lost your mind?"

"Go," Jack encouraged.

"No way!" William was coming at them, his jaw locked in determination. Jack grabbed hold of his arm and pulled him back.

"He's not going to leave here without her," Jack's gaze was steady, yet sad as he stared at the two of them. "He won't be separated from her again, and he'll kill you if you try to stop him. You can't go William. This has to happen," Jack said forcefully.

"We should kill him!" Max snapped.

Jack was pulling a struggling William back, pushing him toward Max as he fought to keep them away. "That will not be possible," Jack muttered, his frustration growing.

"I knew it, you *are* a traitorous bastard. You are on their side, not ours. You're giving her to him!"

"No Max," Arianna's fingers dug into Braith's shirt and skin as she pressed closer. "I gave *myself* to him, long ago."

Max went limp, his mouth dropped as his eyes bugged out of his head. "Aria," William breathed.

She bowed her head for a moment before lifting it to gaze at her brother and friend again. "I'm sorry, but I tried to tell you." She broke off, a single tear slipped down her cheek as she swallowed heavily. "Neither of us intended this, but it's happened, and I can't... I can't let him go."

Braith cradled her cheek for a moment, seeking to give her comfort in this tumultuous situation. "We must go," he urged.

"Wait." Arianna broke away from him. Braith tried to catch hold of her, but she deftly moved out of his reach. Jack caught hold of her, grasping her arms, he held her back as she tried to shove past him. She glared fiercely at Jack as she struggled to get free of his grasp. Braith reclaimed her, taking her gently from Jack's grasp. "Let me say goodbye to my brother!" she protested angrily.

Braith glanced at her brother, he was afraid that William wouldn't let her go. However, Jack had been right about one thing, Braith hated to see Arianna unhappy, and she would be miserable if he didn't allow her to do this. He briskly nodded at Jack, who stepped aside to let William come forward. The siblings embraced while Max glowered at them both.

# CHAPTER TEN

ARIA CLUNG TO BRAITH, burying her head against his back as he carried her through the forest. She was exhausted, her feet throbbed, and all she wanted was to curl up and go to sleep, but Braith insisted that they keep moving, that they get as far from the caves, and that area of the woods, as possible. The moon lit a trail across the forest floor as it crept steadily higher into the night sky.

Though she tried, she was unable to suppress a yawn as she fought against the pull of sleep. She hadn't slept well since she'd last seen him, and now that she was with him again, she knew that she would sleep peacefully and soundly, and she couldn't wait for it. He stopped suddenly, tilting his head back as he studied the night sky. He let her down and placed her onto her feet.

"You have to rest," he said.

She nodded as she pushed back the thick waves of hair that fell across her face. He pulled off his coat and laid it upon the ground. "I wish I could do something more."

Aria managed a small smile for him. "I'm used to sleeping on the ground. Don't worry."

Resignation settled over his features before he unhurriedly came back to her. "Hopefully not for much longer."

"I like the woods. It's where I belong."

He grinned at her, kissing her again. "Yes, it is. But you also like beds."

"I do," she agreed. "And I *love* showers." He chuckled, shaking his head as he stepped back. "Where are we going Braith?"

He knelt beside the coat as he held his hand out to her. She took it and settled down beside him. "There's a place I know where we should be safe."

"And where is this place?"

"About fifty miles from here. I will get us there tomorrow."

"And Jack will know where we are?"

"Yes."

She watched him as he rose to his feet and began to move around the woods. "What is going to happen Braith?"

"I don't know," he answered honestly.

"Are you going to return to the palace?"

He stopped walking as he turned back toward her. "I will not be able to return again Arianna."

Her hands clenched upon her legs as she stared at him in wide eyed disbelief. "It is your family Braith, your heritage."

He was immobile, his jaw locked as he watched the woods behind her. Then, ever so slowly, his gaze came back to her. "*You* are my family now," he said forcefully. "And I will make sure you stay safe."

A startled breath escaped her as tears sprang to her eyes. "Braith," she breathed.

He was back before her in a heartbeat; his hand entwined in her hair, his mouth was supple yet firm against hers. Her toes curled as his kiss sent waves of heat and yearning crashing through her body. She was trembling, shaking as she hugged him. She lost herself to his incredible touch, scent, and feel. His presence was overwhelming, and yet so blissfully soothing. His hands were caressing as they slid over her, pushing aside her clothes to brush over her skin.

Aria's trembling increased; she was inundated with swirling emotions. Her mind and body were spinning as he pushed her onto the coat, his hard body pressing against hers as he came down on top of her. Aria clutched at him, needing something solid in this spiraling, out of control world. The muscles in his arms were shaking as he enveloped her. She could feel his fangs against her mouth, pressing against her as his excitement grew.

Her fingers entwined in his hair, she held him tighter, fighting back the tears of love and joy that burned her eyes. His fingers brushed over her cheeks as he pulled back from her. "Arianna..."

"I love you," she whispered, her fingers skimming over his extended fangs.

His eyes sparked brightly, hunger blazed within his gaze. His lips pressed against hers again, but the driving hunger had left his kiss and had been replaced with a gentleness that left her breathless. She stroked him, guiding his head toward what he desired most right now, her blood.

His mouth skimmed over her skin briefly before he bit down. Aria's hands clenched upon his arms, a low moan escaped her as she felt the tantalizing pull of blood being drawn from her. She closed her eyes, savoring in the delightful feel of him feeding from her, taking nutrition from her body. She drifted in the bliss that rushed over her, consuming her within its cocoon of happiness and awe.

He pulled back from her; his lips were warm against her skin. She was half asleep, drifting in a world of bliss and happiness when he offered her his wrist, allowing her to feed from him and take nourishment and joy from his body also.

ARIA'S GAZE darted rapidly over the buildings as Braith led her down the broken streets of the town. It was a poor town; that much was obvious by the rundown buildings and overly thin animals lurking within the shadows. Braith kept firm hold of her hand as he led her forward. From behind some of the windows she could see people peering out at them, but no one came forth, and the curtains were quickly dropped back into place when she glanced their way.

"What town is this?" she inquired.

Braith shook his head. "I don't know."

He led her down another street, this one containing stores. There were a few people moving about in this area, hurrying from one place to another without stopping to talk to each other. They seemed terrified, beaten, broken by whatever events life had thrown at them. They were the saddest, most heart wrenching people she had ever seen.

"Braith..." He pulled her closer against him as his stride quickened a little more. "These people..."

"Broken."

Aria shuddered at the word, but it was the most appropriate way to describe the lost souls wandering the streets. They turned another corner, hurrying forward as they slipped past houses that were even more worn down by time and poverty. There was a lump of distress in her throat. The towns closer to the palace fared much better than this forgotten wasteland. Here, they seemed to have nothing. There, though they were poor, there were more opportunities for employment, and more money was tossed around by the wealthy residents within the palace towns.

She fought back tears as a young boy darted out of an alleyway. His clothes were no more than rags, cloth was wrapped around his feet for shoes, and he was so dirty that she couldn't discern the true color of his hair. Braith tugged her back as she took a step toward the child, feeling as if she had to do something, but having no idea what she was supposed to do. The boy stopped to stare at her, his eyes gleamed dangerously as he took her in.

"Keep moving Arianna," Braith urged tensely.

"There has to be something..."

"They are not human."

Aria's mouth dropped as she spun toward him. "What?" she gasped.

"They are vampires."

Unease shot through her as she took a step closer to him, pressing against his well muscled body. Her heart hammered, her breath became labored as she wildly glanced around the decrepit streets. She hadn't known that there were vampires that lived like this, and that some vampires had as little as she did within the forest. She'd thought that they were all wealthy, that they all enjoyed the luxurious life that the palace had presented. But these vampires had so very little, and they were starving.

And she appeared to be the only morsel of food around.

"Are they going to come after us?"

"Not if they would like to live."

A chill crept down Aria's spine as he growled the words. He pulled her against him, wrapping his arm around her waist as he held her. They turned another corner; the houses became sparser as the woods began to creep in on them again. Aria glanced over her shoulder, alarmed, and not at all surprised to see that they had attracted a small following. "They're following us," she breathed in horror.

"I know." She swallowed nervously, trying to keep herself under control as her heart thumped and pounded with renewed intensity. It was *her* that they were coming for, but they would kill Braith to get at her. "It's why William couldn't come with us. I couldn't protect you both." She managed a small nod as she bit nervously on her bottom lip. "They won't get anywhere near you Arianna."

"And you?" she whispered.

He shot her a small, arrogant grin that didn't quite reach his eyes. "Impossible."

Aria attempted to take solace in his answer, but there were even more of them back there now. She was grateful for the reassuring weight of her arrows on her back, but she wasn't sure that she had enough in her quiver to even make a dent in the growing population behind them. "Keep your eyes forward," Braith instructed.

She turned back around, her fingers twitched to grasp hold of her bow. "What are we going to do?"

They rounded another corner, the woods pressed closer to them. "You know that tree thing you can do?" Aria nodded. "Why don't you scurry on up there now?"

"I'm not leaving you down here alone!" she protested.

"I'll be fine, Arianna. You have to get up there."

"Braith..."

"Go Arianna, now!" It was the harshest he'd spoken to her in awhile and it left her stunned. Her heart leapt and her mouth went dry as she glanced back at the growing crowd again. Braith was strong, but there were so many of them back there. "Go," he urged, his voice a little kinder.

Aria swallowed heavily, but she didn't refuse him as he nudged her forward. "I'll be fine Arianna, go."

She grasped hold of the first low branch she came across. She threw her arms around the limb, swung her legs over, and maneuvered nimbly up the large oak. She glanced back down at Braith; his head was tilted back as he watched her. She hesitated for a moment, loathe to leave him, but she required a better spot, and a better angle, if she was going to have any hope of taking any of the creatures out with her arrows.

She climbed higher, searching for the branch she could use to attain the next tree. Finding the right one, she ran across the limb. She leapt into the air, feeling a brief moment of elation as the air rushed up around her. Her legs kicked briefly, before she seized hold of the limb of the other tree. Her arms locked around it as she swung easily back into the leafy branches.

Braith moved swiftly across the ground beneath her, keeping his eyes straight as he walked. Aria glanced back as the crowd of fifteen hit the edge of the forest. She had to get the shaking of her hands under control if she was going to continue to make her way through the trees, and not get killed. She darted across another limb, leapt easily into another tree, and then another.

Braith kept pace with her, but the others were gaining on them, and she needed to get a little further ahead. She moved easily, running and leaping until she found a notch in a tree that would be a good place to set up. She pulled an arrow free, placing it easily into her bow. She loved the feeling of power that vibrated up the bow and into her hands. Braith studied her for a moment, shaking his head as he watched her.

She didn't have time to fire the arrow as Braith suddenly launched forward, blurring with speed as he raced at their stalkers. Aria's mouth dropped as he grasped hold of the first one and slammed him into the ground. She was astounded, momentarily dazed by his display of speed and overwhelming power. A muddled squeal escaped his victim, but it was short lived as the victim's throat was crushed beneath the strength of his hand. Three others launched themselves at Braith.

Pushing aside leaves with the tip of her arrow, she took aim at one of the creatures clawing at Braith's back. The arrow released with a distinct twang, it flew straight through the air, striking its target in the back.

The vampire fell off of Braith, squealing as it clawed at its back and squirmed and withered upon the ground. Five pairs of red eyes swung her way as she drew their attention to her location within the tree. She had no fear that they would be able to get her out of the tree; they would have to catch her first in order to do so. Her main concern remained centered upon Braith. Aria quickly drew another arrow, notching it in the bow as she took aim at the next creature that had zeroed in on Braith.

She fired again, this time her arrow flew straight into the creature's heart. It wheeled back, howling as it fell upon the ground and kicked savagely in its death throes. Four of the vampires ran off, fleeing back toward town. Three others became aroused by the scent of blood. Aria recoiled, nausea twisted through her as they fell upon the one she had killed with savage maliciousness.

Braith used their distraction to destroy two more of them, tearing their heads from their bodies before turning his attention to the three now feasting upon their friend. She didn't know what to do as he stalked toward them, bloodlust evident in the stiff set of his shoulders. Aria turned away, unable to watch as he attacked the creatures. She fought the urge to block her ears and flee through the trees in order to escape this atrocity she was trapped in.

She did none of those things as she remained frozen within the tree, shaking with the distress that clung to her. A sharp tug on her foot caught her off guard, nearly ripping her from the tree. She scrambled for purchase; her fingers sought some grip upon the durable limb. Her arm hooked over the branch, just barely saving her from plummeting out of the tree. She was wheezing for breath and terrified, but she managed to gather her wits enough to look down at what had nearly caused her freefall.

A vampire stared back at her, its fangs extended, its eyes red with murderous intent. Aria's jaw almost hit the ground, she had been so upset by the carnage before her that she had missed this approaching threat. It was foolish, stupid, and she was paying for it now as his hand grasped her boot.

Aria swung her other arm up as she attempted to get into a better position in the tree. It jerked down hard on her again, knocking her newly acquired grasp off of the limb. A small gasp of pain escaped her as her hooked arm took the brunt of the violent jerk. She kicked out, trying to knock the creatures grip upon her free, but it refused to relinquish her as its hand slithered up to her ankle. It was surprisingly strong, even in its emaciated state. Or maybe it was starvation that drove it to such levels of strength.

Her arm was aching, her armpit was rubbed raw. Her shoulder felt as if it were going to tear from its socket. She was barely clinging on, barely remaining within the branches of the tree. She kicked out again, trying to knock the creature free as it ripped on her again. A tortured cry escaped from her, a wrenching agony tore through her shoulder as a loud pop filled the air. She couldn't feel her arm as it released its hold upon the limb.

The creature was still holding onto her ankle as she free fell into the air for a few feet. Its grasp kept her in the tree, but it didn't keep her from slamming off of another branch. Her back screamed in protest, the wind was knocked from her. She barely managed to get her good arm up in order to protect her head from the impact of the tree trunk. She was able to twist around and shove herself off the limb as the vampire scrambled to get a better hold on her by moving up her calf. She kicked out, catching the thing beneath its chin, snapping its head back as it hissed and lunged at her as she hung upside down. She kicked out again, knocking it back further. She swung out with her good hand, the full force of her wrath behind the punch. Bone splintered, blood splattered over her as its nose shattered with a loud crack.

The creature howled. It instinctively released her as it grasped hold of its twisted nose. A startled cry escaped her as she freefell into nothing. She struggled to reclaim some hold upon the tree, but it was too late. She tried to keep herself straight, hoping to avoid as many of the branches as possible in her plummet, but they slapped and tore at her.

She heard Braith shout her name, but she couldn't respond to him as she was batted and bounced rapidly back and forth. The branches mercifully gave way as she plummeted toward the ground. Arms encircled her, sheltering her from hitting the ground as Braith took the impact of her body upon himself. A cry of suffering escaped her as he embraced her against his chest.

His hands pushed her tangled hair back from her as he tried to get a look at her. "Arianna," he whispered frantically. "Arianna?"

She took a deep breath, wincing as her bruised body protested the movement. She took a moment to assess the damage that had been done to her. Eventually she was satisfied that though she was wounded, she would heal eventually. "I'm ok," she told him, clenching her teeth as even that small movement caused tenderness to flare through her chest.

"Look at me."

She inhaled a small breath as she forced her eyes open. She blinked in surprise, uncertain about the emotions that surged through her. His much loved eyes were intense, terrified, and a livid shade of red. She didn't know what to make of this stark reminder of what he was, what he was capable of, even if it was all because of her. His gaze searched her face, running rapidly over her, trying to reassure himself that she was, in fact, alright.

Then, his gaze rose to the tree, and the amount of rage that radiated out of him shook her to the marrow of her bones. She didn't look back up at the creature in the tree. He may still be alive right now, but he was as good as dead.

He bit into his wrist, holding his arm out to her as his blood trickled forth. "It will help you heal faster," he informed her.

She hesitated for a brief moment, there had been enough blood today, but she couldn't refuse him. Not when every part of her hurt and not when he was looking at her with that pleading expression. She took his wrist and pressed it against her mouth. His blood was sweet, delicious, and healing as it seeped into her system, flowed through her bruised muscles and dislocated shoulder. When he seemed to think she'd had enough he pulled his wrist away from her. His lips were soft upon her forehead as he released her. "Keep your eyes closed Arianna."

"Braith," she whispered, fighting the chills and tears that burned her eyes.

"Just keep your eyes closed, it will be over quickly."

She closed her eyes, unable to resist obeying him. She forced herself to remain calm as she tried, and failed, to block out the sounds of the ensuing slaughter.

# CHAPTER ELEVEN

ARIANNA CURLED AGAINST HIS CHEST, her hand fisted in his shirt as she slept soundly within his grasp. Braith had hoped that they would be at their destination by now, but the fight with the other vampires, and the tending of her wounds, had put them behind schedule. Night had fallen again and she was exhausted and beaten. His blood would help her to heal faster, but she still moaned every once in awhile, and her face was still scrunched with pain.

He watched her as he moved; awed by the fact that he could even see her; surprised by the fact that he hadn't found her beautiful at first. Yes, she was thinner than he liked, and he had always preferred fairer hair color, and a more refined beauty. But her features, though sharpened by her thinness, were alluring and innocent, and yet possessed a strength of character that was entirely captivating.

They certainly captivated him anyway. He couldn't take his eyes away from her full mouth, slightly pointed nose, and dark eyelashes as they curled against the scattered freckles on her cheeks. When she had been in the palace, out of the rays of the sun, those freckles had almost disappeared completely.

She stirred, her eyelids fluttered open. Her sapphire eyes blazed up at him, an impish smile curved her mouth as she cuddled closer to him. That smile was rare, yet dazzling and devastatingly beautiful. He knew that she had been upset and horrified by what she had witnessed earlier, but she hadn't held it against him, or blamed him for his dark nature. She hadn't turned away from him or turned him away.

"We're almost there," he told her.

She winced as her bad shoulder was jarred. Fury surged through him but he buried it before she could see or sense it. She'd seen enough mayhem today without needing to see anymore from him right now. She stared around the forest, her delicate forehead furrowed in confusion. It didn't look as if the woods were going to end, but they would soon.

"I can walk," she murmured.

"That's ok."

She turned back toward him, her dark eyebrows drawn firmly together. "Your arms must be tired."

"I'm fine Arianna; you weigh as much as a feather."

Displeasure flashed across her face. He bent over her to press a kiss on her nose, hoping to ease her irritation with him. "Are we going to be safe?"

He wished that he could tell her that, yes, they would be. He longed to be able to give her that much, but he couldn't. She had never known safety, had never known a place to call home where she could feel secure, and one day he would give her that, but unfortunately it wouldn't be today. It probably wouldn't be for a long time. Sadness crept into her eyes, she leaned her head against his chest.

"We'll stay together, right?" she asked worriedly.

"Yes."

"That's all that matters then."

His hands clenched around her, he would try to give her the moon if she asked for it, but she had never asked much from him. She didn't require money and jewels, didn't like fancy clothes; she simply desired safety, a place to call home, and him. Unfortunately he didn't have the ability to give her those things right now. One day he would, he promised himself that. The woods gave way, opening onto a house stood within the center of the clearing. The light blazing from the windows illuminated the ground around it.

Arianna's eyes were full of admiration, her hands curled in his shirt as she gazed at the house. It was on stilts, high up in the air, and parts of it were actually built into the trees surrounding the clearing. The sides were all clapboard, though parts of it looked far more weathered than others. The house had been built up since the last time Braith had seen it; it seemed to disappear into the woods behind it now, spreading outward in a ramble of buildings and rooms.

Someone had been busy.

"Wow," Arianna breathed. She wiggled in his arms, and this time he allowed her to drop to her feet. Her rosebud mouth formed a small O as she drank in the sight of the tree house before them. She was most comfortable amongst the trees; this was something spectacular and marvelous to her. "What is this place?"

Braith stared at the growing ensemble of buildings and hallways connecting them. "It belonged to my mother's family originally."

She turned toward him, her gaze questioning. "And now?"

"And now it belongs to my brother in law." Arianna's mouth dropped as she turned back to the tree house.

"Where is your sister?" she inquired.

"You met Natasha when you first arrived in the palace. She didn't leave the palace when Ashby was placed here."

"Not even for her husband?"

Braith slipped his hand into Arianna's, pulling her closer to him. "Not all relationships are like this Arianna, not everyone chooses their partner. Natasha and Ashby were forced together by their families. Natasha is spoiled, rich, and well accustomed to the lap of luxury. Even if she had come to care for Ashby in their time together, she would never leave that behind for him. She wouldn't leave it behind for anyone."

"You left it for me," she managed in a choked voice.

He nodded as he stroked her cheek briefly. "I'd do anything for you." A single tear slipped free. He brushed it away before bending to kiss her.

"Why was Ashby put here?" she asked, her voice choked with emotion.

Braith focused on the ramshackle buildings of the tree house. "During the war with the humans Ashby's family took the side of the humans. As punishment they were all slaughtered, but Ashby was sent to live in exile here, where he was to stay alone, and starving. Though it appears he decided to add even more buildings to the original structure."

"Why was he kept alive?"

"My father felt that this would be a better punishment for him. No luxury, no ready human blood, and no women. Ashby was well known for his love of women and blood. All people, and vampires within the area, were ordered to stay away. There used to be guards here, but they seem to have disappeared, and I have a feeling Ashby is not as weak and deprived as my father had intended. At one time the guards had reported that he was so famished and decimated that he was incapable of move-ment." Apprehension flashed over Arianna's face, she glanced sharply back at the buildings. "I won't let him anywhere near you Arianna."

She nodded but still looked nervous. "Why wouldn't they come here to look for you, if it was your mother's home?"

A shadow passed across one of the curtained windows as it moved across the room. Braith stiffened as he watched Ashby walk through the house. His gate, and purposeful stride, proved what Braith had already suspected. Ashby was no longer too weak to be a threat. "Because Ashby is the reason I was blinded."

Arianna inhaled sharply, her eyes bright in the radiance of the moon. "Braith..."

He took hold of her hand and brought her closer to him. Pulling her hair forward, he draped its thick waves around her neck, trying to mask the scent of her blood, though the sweet smell was impossible to miss. There was little to cover her with though as the summer months didn't allow for much extra clothing. Though it appeared that Ashby had been feeding, Braith didn't know how well, or the last time. Arianna was a temptation that he wasn't sure Ashby wouldn't go after. And Braith didn't want to have to kill him, at least not immediately.

"Come."

She followed behind him, both of her hands clasped around his as a tremor ran through her. He led her up a set of rickety steps, clenching his jaw as the creaking of them made it nearly impossible to keep their pres-ence unknown. The stairs swayed as they stepped off them and onto a wobbly deck that he wasn't entirely certain would hold up beneath their weights. He wouldn't have been surprised if Ashby had set up booby traps. When Arianna tried to walk beside him, he pushed her back with an admonishment to walk only where he had. She frowned fiercely at him, but for once didn't argue.

Braith wondered again where the guards were. He should have left Arianna in the woods, but even if he couldn't sense the guards, that didn't mean they weren't still out there. He couldn't take that chance with her life. He held his arm out, keeping her behind him as he tried the knob. He wasn't surprised to find it locked.

He waited for a moment, trying to decide if he should break in, or knock. He glanced back at Arianna, she was biting her bottom her lip, and sweat had begun to form along her hairline. He squeezed her hand for reassurance, but he could tell it did little to appease her.

In the end, he decided to knock. There was something about this situation that he found strange and offsetting, for some reason he felt that knocking might be the bigger element of surprise here.

From inside he could hear the approaching sound of footsteps; a faint whistling pierced the air. Braith was jarred for a moment, thrown back to a time when they had all lived together in the palace. Ashby had always whistled, not a loud piercing whistle, but a melodious rhythm that had drifted cheerfully through the halls. It had been lively and carefree, as upbeat and easygoing as the man that issued it. All of the women had loved Ashby; they had thrown themselves at his feet, enchanted by his good looks, and charming demeanor.

Now that whistle drifted easily through the air, lazy and casual, not at all the sound that a prisoner fighting for their lives should be making. This whistle was happy, easy, and so unbelievably joyful that it set Braith's teeth on edge. The two of them had once been good friends, more than brothers-in-law, but actually brothers. Then Ashby had betrayed them, Braith had been blinded, and their friendship had been forever severed. Ashby was supposed to have been punished for that betrayal, but it was more than obvious that he was not serving that punishment anymore.

The door was flung open and Braith came face to face with the man who had once been his best friend, and was now one of his greatest enemies. Ashby was grinning stupidly; his eyes were bright with merriment before reality began to sink in. He looked much as Braith remembered; he had not wasted away, did not appear starved, and in fact appeared to be a little heavier than he had been in the palace.

Then, Ashby's grin faded as disbelief, alarm, and finally terror flitted over his face. Braith was moving forward even as Ashby was trying to slam the door shut. The solid wood bounced off of his hand, slamming back against the wall with a loud crash that shattered wood and caused Arianna to gasp loudly. Ashby was scrambling backward, trying to escape when Braith seized him by the throat, lifted him up, and smashed him into the wall with enough force to shatter the plaster.

He hadn't seen Ashby in a hundred years, but the knife of betrayal that stabbed through him was just as fresh and sharp as it had been back then. This had been a bad idea. Braith had come here knowing that no one would look for him here; he had come here thinking that Ashby may still have contacts that would help him keep Arianna safe. He had come here expecting Ashby to be paying for his sins, not thoroughly enjoying his life.

The full force of his hatred for Ashby was slamming rapidly through him, and all of his reasons for being here vanished in an instant.

Now he just wanted to kill him. Ashby's bright green eyes filled with terror, his hands clawed at Braith's arm, trying to dislodge Braith's brutal grip. His heels kicked against the wall as a choked grunt escaped him. Braith's fangs were fully extended; he pressed his face closer to Ashby's, enjoying the growing fear radiating from him.

"Hello brother," Braith sneered.

Ashby choked, his movements became wilder as Braith pressed down remorselessly. "Braith." Arianna's stunned whisper barely pierced through the red haze of his fury. He turned toward her, trying to make her out through the cloud that blurred his vision. "Braith."

Braith clenched down more forcefully and then he eased his grip. Arianna knew exactly what he was capable of, but he couldn't bring himself to kill in cold blood in front of her. He may kill Ashby later, but he would require more of an excuse than the fact that his ex brother-in-law had opened the door. He shoved Ashby roughly back as he stepped away from him.

Ashby's hand went to his throat; he staggered away from the wall, his gaze hooded as he stared at Braith. Arianna stood back, her hands clenched on the bow at her side. He hadn't realized she had pulled it out until now, and she wasn't going to put it away if the stubborn set of her jaw meant anything. She stared defiantly back at him for a moment before her angry gaze slid to Ashby.

Ashby's forehead was furrowed as his attention drifted to Arianna. Then, his gaze slid over her, raking her from head to toe. The confusion in his bright green eyes was apparent as he turned back to Braith. "Where are the guards?" Braith inquired his voice low and ferocious.

Ashby swallowed, he rubbed his throat again, but he didn't speak. Braith grabbed hold of his shoulders, slamming him off the wall as he shook him roughly. Ashby staggered but quickly caught his balance again. His lips curled into a sneer, his fangs extended but he didn't come at Braith, he was too smart for that. Braith was older, stronger, and well sated.

"Where are the guards?" he demanded again.

Ashby straightened his shoulders, fixing his shirt as he stepped away from the wall. He had always been meticulously dressed and groomed. "Dead." Braith nodded as he glanced around the large room, he had already expected that answer.

His mother's family had once had the home finely appointed with classical furniture, and works of art. All of those things had been stripped from the house when Ashby had been banished here. Now, though the room was still fairly bare, Braith was not surprised to see that Ashby had managed to find a few nicer things to decorate it with. Ashby had always appreciated the finer things in life; he would find a way to incorporate them into his home.

"Who speaks with the guards from the palace when they call?"

"I do."

"So you discovered the code word, and killed them."

It had not been a question, but Ashby answered anyway. "Yes."

"When will someone from the palace be getting into contact again?"

"Not until tomorrow morning. They checked in about an hour ago. I won't tell you the password." Braith hadn't thought he would. Ashby would stay alive for as long as it was necessary. When Ashby's gaze slid back toward Arianna he stepped in between them. "She's human."

"Very astute of you," Braith retorted.

Ashby's eyes narrowed on Braith. "Why are you here Braith? What are *you* doing with a human? Why is she not wearing a leash?"

Arianna bristled as she stepped forward. "I am *not* a blood slave."

"Arianna." Braith pushed her back, trying to keep her as far from Ashby as possible.

Ashby was studying her in surprise and disbelief. Then his gaze drifted down to her shoulder. Her loose shirt had slid down to reveal the marks that marred her porcelain skin. Hunger flashed through his eyes, but something even more flitted across his features. "You're not a blood slave, and you're not a palace woman, yet you nurture him?"

Arianna's hands twitched upon her bow. Braith wouldn't put it past her to draw an arrow and shoot him just to make herself feel better. He pulled the collar of her shirt up, stroking her skin for a brief moment before he covered the marks. Her eyes fired with love, a smile curved her mouth.

"How did you know her shirt was down?" Braith turned back to Ashby, a small smile curved his lips. Ashby's mouth dropped, his eyes widened as realization staggered him. "You can see!" Braith just shrugged in response. "What? How? I don't understand." Ashby's attention turned back to Arianna, his dark blond hair spilled across his forehead as he shook his head. "I thought your eyesight was gone for good."

"Do you have a place where she can lie down?" Braith inquired, unwilling to even begin to ease some of Ashby's curiosity and questions.

"I'm not leaving you," Arianna protested.

"You're exhausted."

"I'm fine Braith."

"Arianna..."

"No, I am not leaving you alone with *him*!" she retorted sharply.

"What the hell," Ashby whispered as his head bounced back and forth like a ping pong ball between them.

"Shut up!" Braith snapped at him. "Arianna..."

"I'm fine Braith, really. I slept on the way here, remember. I don't want to leave you alone, or *be* alone right now." Her response was so honest, so vulnerable that it tugged at his heart. He didn't like her anywhere near Ashby, but he couldn't force her away. Especially not now that he realized beneath her defiant expression and posture, she was terrified.

"Sit down."

He wasn't surprised when she didn't move but simply stood immobile with her hands clenched around the bow. "Jesus," Ashby muttered. "What is going on Braith? Why are you here? And what *is* she to you!?"

"That's not your concern," Braith informed him. "Who were you expecting?"

"I don't know what you mean," Ashby replied, trying to appear nonchalant but failing miserably.

"You were whistling when you opened the door, you weren't worried that there may be a threat on the other side. *Who* were you expecting?"

Ashby tilted his chin to glare at Braith. "You have your secrets and I have mine," he responded crisply.

"I have my secrets but I can, and will, tear your eyes out." Braith pushed him back, pressing him firmly against the wall. "I already owe you one Ashby; you think I won't take great pleasure in blinding you before drawing your death out."

Ashby turned toward Arianna, his brows quirked upward. "She doesn't look too pleased by that notion."

"I don't have to watch," Arianna informed him tautly.

Braith gave her an approving nod before turning his attention back to Ashby. The knock on the door snapped all of their heads around. Ashby opened his mouth to shout a warning, but Braith seized hold of his throat, cutting his cry swiftly off. Before Ashby could react Braith delivered a crushing blow that immediately knocked him out. Arianna was gaping at him, her eyes dazed with astonishment. He placed his finger to his lip, directing her to remain silent as he made his way toward the door. He heard the arrow being knocked back against the bow, but he didn't look back.

He pulled aside the curtain a little. He couldn't see who was on the porch, but he was satisfied that it was only one person. He threw the door open, not at all surprised to see a girl standing outside. She was, however, surprised to see him. A small cry escaped her as Braith seized hold of her arm and jerked her into the house.

# CHAPTER TWELVE

Aria sat on the edge of the couch with her hands clasped before her, but she could grab the bow and quiver by her feet in an instant. Ashby was holding a rag to his cut lip. Aria leaned forward, not liking the look in Ashby's bright green eyes as he watched Braith.

He was exceptionally good looking in an easy going, charming way. His dark blond hair was shaggy as it fell forward in waves across the carved planes of his face. There was an air of indifference surrounding him, and yet Aria sensed that there was something more to him, something that even Braith didn't know about. Something that Ashby had managed to keep hidden from everyone that had ever known him.

She didn't know why she was so convinced of this; perhaps it was years of learning to read people within the forest. But she couldn't shake the feeling that there was far more to Ashby than met the eye.

The young girl sat across from him, her brown eyes darting frantically around as she nervously watched them. She was pretty, with dark hair that fell in thick waves about her delicate shoulders. She was older than Aria, about twenty two or three in appearance. Though there was no way to know her real age, as she was not human. A fact that had been made clear when she'd attempted to attack Braith, only to be quickly rebuffed.

He had tied her hands behind her back, and then secured her to a beam in the ceiling with enough rope to allow her to keep her hands down. Her legs were also tied, with another length of rope that ran to a different beam. Aria was edgy, nervous about this situation, uncertain as to what they were doing here, and what Braith planned for these two.

Ashby appeared just as uncertain as he watched Braith suspiciously. "What have you gotten yourself into Braith?" he inquired.

"I don't see how that is any of your concern."

She felt the spark of curiosity that raced through Ashby as his eyes raked over her again. Aria shifted, hating the way he continued to look at her like she was something to eat, or an oddity that he couldn't explain. Aria forced herself not to squirm beneath his scrutiny, forced herself to steadfastly return his gaze.

"You've come to *me* Braith; that makes it my concern. You have brought whatever trouble you are in into *my* world. I have a right to know what that is."

Braith turned to him, but his jaw was taut, and Aria was well aware of the fact that he was not going to talk to Ashby. She was just as curious as Ashby was, just as puzzled as to what Braith had planned, but if Braith was unwilling to say it in front of Ashby than she wasn't going to press him. "This isn't your world Ashby, it's your prison. Or at least it was supposed to be. Who is the girl?"

"Who is *your* girl?" Ashby retorted.

A low growl of frustration escaped Braith. The hair on Aria's neck and arms stood on end as he stalked toward Ashby. She was afraid that he was going to kill Ashby; apparently Ashby felt the same way as he recoiled from Braith's approach. Aria leapt to her feet to stop Braith when the girl charged at her with a violent hiss. Aria spun, but she was caught off guard by the girl's sudden attack. Taken aback by the brutality the girl radiated, Aria fell back as she lunged forward with a ferocious snarl, red eyes, and hooked fingers.

She was defenseless, having left her bow by the sofa. Reacting on instinct alone, she slammed a fist into the girl's cheek, putting the full force of her weight behind it. Aria's blow barely did anything to affect the vampire, but the ropes caught suddenly, roughly jerking her back. The girl fell on her ass; a frustrated cry escaped her as she slammed her hands on the floor.

Braith was before her, his hands grasping hold of her arms. "Are you ok?" he demanded. Aria swallowed heavily as she tried to calm the frantic beat of her heart. "Arianna?"

"I'm fine. I'm fine," she assured him.

He grasped hold of her chin, turning her face toward him. His eyes were dark and simmering with the barely contained bloodlust that pulsated through him. She had seen that look a few times from him before, but it still scared her, mainly because she knew there was nothing that she could do to stop whatever it was he had in mind. "Braith..."

But it was not the girl that Braith took his anger out on, it was *her*. His mouth seized hers in a desperate, needy way that left her staggered and shaken. He took firm possession of her, pulling her roughly against him. Though she was originally shocked into immobility by his fervent desire, she felt herself melting against him. She gave into his wild desire, mainly because she couldn't refuse him anything, but also because she needed this as badly as he did. His hand was firm in her hair; his fingers cradled her head as he deepened the kiss. His tongue was hot and heady as it swept into her mouth.

He reluctantly pulled away from her; his arms trembled as he rested his forehead against hers. Aria couldn't catch her breath as she struggled to calm the hum of passion his volatile kiss had ignited. She gripped his strong, corded arms as she sought to keep herself grounded in this strange new world and the overwhelming sensations that he evoked in her.

"I need you to go into the other room."

"Braith..."

"Just for a minute Arianna, I don't want you to see this."

Disbelief and disgust tore through her as she realized what he planned to do. They were outnumbered here, between Ashby and the girl they were under constant threat of attack. But the girl was tied up, defenseless. It wasn't right. She was shaking her head, trying to get words out, but he was already pushing her toward the door of another room.

"Braith wait." She frantically grasped at his arms. "Don't do this, not like this Braith."

"I'm not going to kill her."

"But..."

"It's ok Arianna; go on now, just for a moment."

She was frowning at him, but he had already managed to navigate her through the doors and into a room that appeared to be a library. Braith glanced around; displeasure crossed his features as he took in the vast array of books. "Braith?"

He kissed her quickly before spinning away from her. "I just need some time alone with them, with *him*. Stay in here."

She didn't have time to argue with him as he closed the door. Exasperation and disbelief surged through when she heard the click of the lock pop into place. Her hands fisted, she bit her bottom lip in frustration as she fought the urge to race at the door and pound on it until he opened it again. It would appear childish, she knew that, but she also knew that she was *not* going to be confined to this damn room, and she was *not* going to let him order her around like this.

She made her way rapidly through the other rooms. As she moved through the ramshackle house the rooms and doorways became more haphazard. It was easy to tell what had been the original house, and what the newest additions to the massive tree structure were. The floor creaked beneath her, but she wasn't worried that it might collapse, it seemed solid enough. She passed by an extended version of the library, a rather large and surprisingly well equipped kitchen, a den, three bedrooms, and two bathrooms with showers. Blessed showers, that if they were here long enough, and things settled down, she was going to enjoy.

Then, there were the empty rooms, apparently built just to keep Ashby busy during his time of confinement. The additions weaved deeper through the forest, branching off into new and different angles. Limbs from the trees had been used for support and incorporated into the rambling structure. Despite its empty air, and somewhat lonely feel, there was something about the strange house that intrigued her. She had always been more at home within the trees than anywhere else; this was the kind of place that she could live in. This was the kind of place that she could one day call home. It was a strange realization, one that was astounding even to her, as she'd never thought about having a stable home, but it felt right somehow.

She came to the end of the structure, stopping as she came face to face with the wall before her. Frustration filled her, she had been hoping that this meandering labyrinth somehow came back around on itself, but it didn't. Fighting the urge to kick the wall, Aria fisted her hands and spun back around. She yearned to be with Braith, but she wasn't going to be relegated to this small role, she was *not* going to be ordered about and hidden away like a child that couldn't fend for herself.

She *could* fend for herself; in fact she was far better at it than almost anyone else she knew.

Maybe she wasn't as quick and strong as a vampire, but she had her own set of skills that elevated her above most humans. She stormed back through the rooms, determined to have it out with Braith. She was making her way through the kitchen when he appeared in the doorway. She could see the barely contained tension simmering beneath his surface; sense the thin thread of control that he had over himself.

Aria froze as she took him in. He was being pushy and overbearing, but for the first time she glimpsed the fear he was trying to keep from her. The fear that he wasn't going to be able to keep her safe, that he would lose her. She also saw the strain he was going through at having to face Ashby.

Braith's eyes were smoldering, his shoulders rigid. His thirst was nearly palpable within the room. He had fed recently, but the stress of their current situation was clearly wearing on him. She felt that he hadn't even realized how strenuous and draining this would be on him.

She couldn't promise him that they would be safe, that they would make it through this, but she could help to ease the burning thirst throbbing from him. She pulled her shirt down to bare the fresh marks upon her skin to him. His eyes sparked with hunger, she could see the press of his fangs against the inside of his clamped mouth. A muscle twitched in his cheek. She didn't jump when he slammed his hand against the wall, causing a few pots within one of the cabinets to shift and fall with a muted rattle.

"It's too soon. No."

The words were grated at her, harsh with the exertion he was using to maintain control of himself. "I can take it."

"You were hurt pretty badly today. No."

He was going to fight her, she knew that. No matter how much he needed this, her safety was number one with him. And if he felt that he was going to harm her, or that this would be a danger to her, than he wasn't going to do it. But she was far more stubborn then he was, and she *wanted* this just as badly as he *needed* it. She was beginning to realize that she craved him feeding from her as much as he craved her blood. Despite the brief pain the experience brought her, it also brought moments of pure, unadulterated joy. It was thrilling and wondrous to be able to sustain him with blood, her body. It was exhilarating to have him on her, in her, gaining strength from her. She may not be the only one that he could gain such nourishment from, but she was the only one that he wanted to feed from anymore. If he was going to have any sort of relief, she was the only one that could give it to him.

Her heart thumped with the excitement of that knowledge as she moved toward him. "Arianna."

His voice was a soft plea but she couldn't back down from this. He may not feel it was safe to feed from her right now, but he had to. She stopped before him. He pulled her shirt up but she caught hold of his hand, resting it against her chest, over top of her heartbeat.

"Do you feel that?" His eyes were dark, stormy as he raised his gaze to hers. She knew that he could feel it, it was impossible not to feel the forceful beat of it. "It's yours. *I* am yours Braith. I'm strong, I can handle this; take what you have to from me."

Though he was still vibrating with hunger, his eyes were also filled with awe. His fingers curled against her chest, he bent to kiss her forehead, then her cheek, and ear. "I am yours also Arianna, never doubt that."

"I never will," she vowed.

His hand curled in her hair, caressing her tenderly. Though his finger trailed over the old marks, he didn't bite her, but simply stood over her, soothing and stroking her. He shuddered, his muscles rippled against her, she felt his weakening. He kissed her neck gingerly, the hard press of his fangs caused her heart to lurch with excitement. A low moan of pleasure escaped, her knees nearly buckled as he bit into her, joining them once again. She was clinging to him, shaking as waves of ecstasy crashed over her. No matter how awful the world around them was, this exchange, this one moment of perfect bliss, and pleasure, was worth every horror she was certain was coming their way, if it wasn't already here.

He nuzzled her as he licked the lingering drops of blood from her skin. He hadn't taken as much as he normally would have. "You must take more..."

"I'm fine."

"Braith, you have to stay strong, take more."

"It is too soon for you."

She swallowed heavily, trying to rid herself of the lump forming in her throat. Though the next words were going to kill her, she managed to strangle them out. "Then you must go to someone else."

His hands stilled on her, he lifted her face to him. She couldn't hide the sorrow that such a thought caused her. It would be awful for him to turn to someone else for this, awful for her, but he *had* to feed. He had to stay strong, especially now, and she couldn't give him all that he required right now. Maybe one day, when there wasn't so much pressure and strain on him, she could be enough. But that wasn't today, and it probably wasn't going to be anytime soon. They both had to accept the fact that he would have to go somewhere else, to someone else, and there was nothing that either of them could do to stop it from happening.

"That thought doesn't make you happy."

"Of course not, but I would rather you stay strong than have you get hurt because you were hungry, or weak."

"I will not be either one of those things."

"Braith..."

"I will find other ways Arianna. I will substitute what you cannot give me with animals."

"Is that the same?" she whispered.

He smiled as he kissed her nose lightly. "It may not taste as good, but it is just as nourishing. Nothing tastes as good as you." She shook her head at him as he pushed her hair back. "You're the most delicious thing I've ever encountered."

Aria shuddered; a thrill of pleasure ran down her spine as her body swayed closer to his. "You don't have to say that," she breathed.

"It's true." His hand was on her neck, his palm pressed over the marks there. *His* marks. "I don't want anyone but you Arianna. The idea of it is repulsive to me, especially since I know it upsets you."

"I won't let you suffer."

"I will not suffer and I will not turn to someone else. You are mine, you will *always* be mine." His voice rang with possessiveness, she could feel his tension spiking again. It was the first time she realized that it wasn't just this entire situation that had him so out of sorts, but also *her*. It was a frightening and disconcerting realization, she didn't know how to help him, how to ease the stress thrumming through him. "The thought of you turning to someone else, for anything, makes me want to destroy this entire place, makes me want to shred someone limb from limb. I wouldn't inflict such hurt upon you by using another to sustain me."

She stared at him in surprise, disturbed by the rapid change she sensed in him. Disturbed by the fact that she was a large part of the insta-bility she sensed growing inside of him. "I would never do that," she promised. He was dark, remorseless, and distant in a way that he hadn't been since she had first met him within the palace walls. For a moment it seemed as if he didn't see her, as if he was trapped in the thought of her with another man. "Braith, I would never turn to someone else. You are the only one that has *ever* made me feel like this."

He swallowed heavily, she didn't think he was aware of the fact that his sudden instability had caused his fangs to sprout forth again. He closed his eyes for a moment, when he opened them again she was relieved to see a softening in his gaze. "I know Arianna. I know you wouldn't."

"Never Braith. *Never.*" She hoped that her insistence would help to get through to him, but she still sensed something dark and turbulent beneath his calm exterior. His hand was tense upon her neck, his grip almost bruising. "The thought is repulsive to me."

"I know."

"Then why do you seem so troubled? So angry?"

He looked startled by her observation, his gaze darted to his hand. He shook his head, his eyes filled with a self hatred that rattled her. He pulled his hand away as he took a small step back from her. "I'm sorry Arianna; I didn't mean to hurt you."

"You didn't," she assured him quickly, terrified by the strange gap she felt expanding between them. A gap she didn't understand, just as she didn't understand what was going on with him. She enfolded his hand in hers. "Braith you could never hurt me."

He didn't look appeased by her words. He didn't even look as if he believed them. "We should return."

"Braith, what is wrong?" she demanded, becoming frightened by the strange air that now encompassed him.

He grabbed hold of her, pulling her against him. A small gasp of surprise escaped her as he fell to his knees before her. He wrapped his arms around her waist as he rested his head against her stomach. "You humble me Arianna. I don't deserve you; I did nothing to earn your love, or the gift of sight that your presence has brought back to my life." Aria was frozen, astounded at the picture of the most powerful creature she had ever known, her prince, on his knees before her, broken by the anguish pouring from him. Anguish she did not understand.

Tears spilled from her, her chest constricted in distress. She buried her hands in his hair as a low cry escaped her. She bowed over him, cradling him against her, fighting not to give into the powerful sobs threatening to escape her. He was humbled by her, he felt that he didn't deserve her, and yet if it hadn't been for him she would still be dead and lost inside. She may well *be* dead if he hadn't been there to intervene. If it wasn't for him, she never would have known the joy of love, the wonder of things that she'd never understood until he walked into her life. If it wasn't for him, she never would have learned what life was truly about, she would have lost out on so much without his love to save her.

She slid to her knees before him, clinging to him as he enveloped her, rocking her against him, holding her, and touching her so reverently that she could barely breathe through the love swirling and building within her. His presence overwhelmed her; it floored her, and rocked her with its intensity. His hands were in her hair; his mouth and tongue had fierce possession of hers. His kiss was passionate, burning with a desperation that left her shaken. For the first time she realized that though he didn't pressure her, didn't push her toward anything, there was something else that he wanted even more than her blood.

He also wanted her body.

Aria shuddered, desire pooled through her. It was something that she hadn't been ready for, something she hadn't given because circumstances always seemed to separate them. But even though they were on the run, adrift in a world that provided no security, there were no barriers between them anymore. She didn't even care that they were kneeling on a kitchen floor right now; she was so swept up in the aching desire pulsating through her.

He pulled away from her, shaking as he held her. "Arianna," he moaned.

"I understand. I know what you need." But though she said the words, she wasn't sure they were right. She knew he craved this as badly as she did, but she wasn't entirely certain that it would be enough. She sensed that he may require more than just her blood and her body. He already had her heart and soul; she didn't know what else she could give him to ease the distress she sensed growing within him.

"Arianna." His voice was a low groan of torment. "You are so innocent. So sweet..."

"I'm not that sweet."

His smile was strained, his eyes dark and tortured. "True," he agreed. She grinned at him, sensing the easing in his mood that she had been hoping for. "There is so much you don't know about me though. So much that you could never understand. There are things that I have done..."

She placed her fingers over his mouth, silencing him. "Don't Braith. You're not going to scare me away; you are not going to *drive* me away. You are not your father, you are not Caleb."

"I am a killer."

"I have killed also," she managed to choke out.

"In self-defense. I killed for pleasure, for joy." She tried to turn away from him; she had no desire to hear this. She knew what he was, knew what he was capable of; she had witnessed the full force of his brutality earlier. He grabbed hold of her though, pulling her back toward him. "You have to hear this Arianna."

"I understand Braith; you don't have to do this."

"I do, because you *don't* understand. I never killed for pleasure, never killed for the joy of it." She frowned at him, not understanding where he was going with this. "Until Jack took you away from me."

Aria recoiled, the color drained from her face. He was right, she didn't understand this. He had told her about the blood slaves he'd taken after her escape, and though she hadn't asked, she'd assumed that he hadn't killed them. The Braith she knew was kind, caring, overly protective, and as willing to die for her as he was willing to kill for her, but he was not vicious. And this conversation was taking a turn toward cruelty that she hadn't expected from him.

"And then I lost myself to the pleasure of the blood, the pleasure of sex, and the pleasure of the death." She felt nauseous. She was going to throw up. He was a killer, she understood that. There were other women before her, she knew that. He was over nine hundred years old for crying out loud, she'd be a fool to think there hadn't been other women, but she didn't care to hear about them. And she didn't want to hear about him glutting himself on them, in thriving on destroying them. He leaned closer to her, his eyes burned with a strange fire. "I did not enjoy it for long Arianna."

She shook her head, forcing herself not to recoil from him. She loved him, but how did she assimilate the monster he was describing to the man before her? "Why?" she managed to croak out.

"Because for brief moments of time I was almost able to forget you, but I eventually realized that I didn't enjoy it and it truly didn't help."

She stifled a moan as she closed her eyes. Guilt stained her soul and twisted in her stomach. It was not her fault that he had done those things. *He* had chosen to kill, but her absence had been the catalyst that sent him spiraling over the edge. "Why are you telling me this?" she whispered.

His hand was gentle as he gripped her chin. "Because you must know."

She shook her head in denial. She loved him, she truly did, but now she felt ragged and raw. He had starkly reminded her of things that she didn't like to recall, reminded her of the fact that, though she had no one to compare him to, there were probably hundreds, if not thousands, that he would be comparing her to. He had also harshly reminded her of the fact that he was a monster, or at least he had the potential to be. He would never harm her, but what would he do to someone else that stood in his way?

She knew the answer to that, and it would be something immediate, and violent.

"Arianna, you have to understand what it is that I am saying to you." She blinked, her eyes burned with tears, but she was confused as to why he kept pushing this. "I can't lose you again; it sent me into a dark spiral. It snapped something inside of me, turned me into something evil and twisted. It wrecked me. I upheld my promise, I didn't reclaim any blood slaves after the last time I saw you. I couldn't, the thought of them was repulsive to me. But I cannot lose you from my life again, many will not survive it."

"You're not going to," she promised.

His hands were on her face, his eyes forceful and smoldering. "Whatever this is between us, it's something that I don't understand, it's something strong, intense, pure, and yet consuming. It is something magnificent and precious, but it can also turn me into something horrendous. Losing you would drive me mad. I am one of the strongest of our kind, I am a prince, and my blood is powerful, old, untainted. If I snap, if I go on a rampage, I will destroy many people before I am stopped. *If* I am stopped."

"Braith I will never leave you," she promised.

"You are *human* Arianna. As long as you stay human you will be mortal, at risk of death."

"Braith..."

"I can't take the chance of you being killed. I can't risk that."

Realization was cold and vile as it hit her with the force of a brutal slap. He did covet more than just her blood, more than her body even.

He wanted her *life*. It was the only thing she couldn't give him right now, if ever, but seeing the amount of stress he was under, she wasn't sure she would be able to stop him from taking it by force.

# CHAPTER THIRTEEN

ARIANNA WAS STILL pale and shaken. She hadn't spoken since he'd made his revelation to her, she had barely even moved. Every once in awhile, she would stare at him, her eyes would darken, and her hands would begin to tremble in her lap once more. She was the strongest human he had ever encountered, perhaps even the strongest *being* he had ever come into contact with, but his confession, his openness, had rattled her completely.

As had his intention to take her humanity from her.

It was not something he looked forward to doing, but it was something he *had* to do. Something he was *going* to do. He realized that now, he just hoped that eventually she would be willing. He didn't know how he would handle it if she wasn't, didn't know how he would handle it if she remained human. But he couldn't take the chance of losing her again. When he thought back to the things he had done after she left him, he was repulsed by his actions. He was shocked by the depths of his depravity, shocked by his fervent need to lose himself in blood, sex, and death in order to try to forget her. He'd never experienced the ravenous brutality that had encompassed him before then. It had ensnared him within a web of death that had done little to ease the torment residing within his soul.

A torment that she had inflicted and only she had eased. He'd come to realize that it would only ever be her that could pull him back from that dark place. A place he'd entered a few times today, slaughtering and killing anyone that had posed any kind of threat to her life. She could pull him back from the brink of madness; she gave him some kind of control over himself. But it was a control that was unraveling rapidly.

He knew that, he could feel it within the marrow of his bones. She would be his undoing, as he would be hers.

She was everything to him; she was his light in a world that had been black before her. She couldn't stay human, and he wasn't sure that he could change her. He'd heard of it being done before, but had never witnessed it, and had never attempted such a feat himself. It was risky, many didn't survive.

He was determined that she would.

"Braith." Ashby was watching him warily. Yet, there was something in his eyes, something almost knowing. Braith stopped pacing, tilting his head as he studied his enemy. "What have you gotten yourself into?"

Braith strode toward the window. He pulled the curtain back to peer out on the dawning day. He didn't expect Jack to make it today, but perhaps by nightfall. "Have you forsaken your right to the throne?"

He turned as the young vampire girl made a startled sound. He'd tightened her bonds, making it almost impossible for her to move. Arianna's pleas had saved the woman's life; it wouldn't take much for him to change his mind though. "You are the prince?" she questioned in awe.

"I am no prince," Braith growled at her.

The girl tugged against the ropes, struggling to break free. Arianna watched her with fascination, but he could see the deep turmoil churning behind her eyes. She didn't like what he'd done to the girl, but she didn't protest it either. She seemed resigned to the fact that the woman would remain tied up.; she wasn't resigned to this situation though as her eyes came back to him.

"So the son has turned his back on his father. Caleb must be thrilled," Ashby purred. "What must Jericho think?" Braith remained silent; Ashby would learn soon enough that Jericho had abandoned his place in the palace before Braith had. "The palace streets will run red with blood if Caleb ever ascends the throne."

Braith snorted in disgust as he shook his head at Ashby. "Do you really think my father is ready to hand over his rule?"

"I think that Caleb will try to take it from him, when he is ready to."

"You may be right."

"It will be horrific and violent."

"It will," Braith agreed.

Frustration flashed across Ashby's handsome features. "You *know* what will happen with Caleb in charge Braith. You *know* what he will do. This pretty little thing that you've brought in here, you *know* what Caleb would do to her!"

"He'll have to find her first."

Ashby climbed to his feet. Stepping forward, he halted as he was brought up by the constraints wrapped around him. "Braith, this is *Caleb* we are talking about. He will raze every town in order to find you, in order to make sure that you do not come back and try to reclaim your birthright. You think your *father* is a sadistic son of a bitch, he has nothing on Caleb."

"I know my family Ashby," Braith's voice was low, deadly.

Ashby shook his head. "You have no idea of the stain that rests on their souls," Ashby told him. "Of their cruelty and immorality."

"And you do?" Braith inquired.

He pondered the question. "We didn't turn against your family because mine was hoping to take over, or because we cared about the humans." Arianna glared at Ashby. "We wanted nothing of power Braith, you know that. We were an easy going lot, all of us. Power was never our goal; fun was all that we ever required, freedom, no restraints. It wasn't power we sought Braith, it wasn't to save the human race."

Braith folded his arms firmly over his chest, leaning back on his heels as he studied his brother-in-law with disdain. "Then what did you want?" he demanded.

"Peace Braith, we simply sought peace. Things were well enough before the war. So what if vampires didn't mosey about openly in public? Who cared that we had to keep our identities secret? Not me, not my family, not you. It's not as if we didn't have fun, not as if we didn't take whatever we required, whenever we required it anyway. Why upset the balance? Why take a chance that it could all go wrong? That it could be even worse afterward?

"And it *was* worse afterward. For everyone. We were relegated to these positions that none of us wanted. You had always been the prince amongst our people, but you know you never liked it, and until the war you never thought seriously about what it meant. Do you think I enjoyed being married to that bitch sister of yours? Natasha could suck the fun out of the happiest fellow. Which I was, until that time."

Braith was not surprised to find Arianna enrapt by what Ashby was saying. He wanted to remove her from this room, and Ashby's poison, but he knew that she wouldn't go. Besides, Ashby was right; Natasha was cold, hateful, and almost as twisted as Caleb himself. And though Ashby was fun loving, and more than enjoyed his share of blood, he had never relished in the death as so many members of Braith's family did. As *Braith* had.

"We didn't require power Braith, we only wanted to be free. Apparently you have decided the same, or else you wouldn't be here."

Braith would like the same thing, but he wanted Arianna to be free even more. He aspired to have her experience a world that she had never known, one that was safe and secure, one where she didn't have to fear his father and brother, one where she did not have to fear *him*. "Will they be coming here Braith?" Ashby inquired worriedly.

"I don't know," he admitted.

Ashby jerked against his ties as he lurched forward. "You can't leave me here if they do! I am sorry for what happened to you, I always did like you; you know that. You were an unfortunate casualty Braith; you were not the intended victim. Your father was."

"That is supposed to make things better?" Braith barked.

"You care nothing for the man either," Ashby retorted. "I lived within those walls, I knew you from a young age; I know what that bastard did to you! I know what you endured at his hands!"

Arianna slowly turned toward him, she was still abnormally pale, and there was a vacancy in her eyes that shook him. Though he hadn't completely kept the abuse he'd taken from his father from her, he hadn't elaborated upon it either. She didn't have to know about that horror on top of all of the others she had endured. "Braith?"

He shook his head; he wasn't going to go into details about it, not now. "They are going to come here?" the vampire girl croaked. When no one answered, she lurched forward, a terrified scream erupting from her. She ripped and jerked against her bonds, her head whipped back and forth as she continued to scream wildly. Arianna recoiled, the woman was wild, crazed, her fangs had extended, and her eyes were a vicious shade of red.

The woman could very well get free if she continued on this way, and she was going to go after Arianna if she did. "Don't!" Arianna cried launching to her feet as Braith strode toward the crazed vampire. She stumbled forward, unnaturally clumsy as her foot got caught up on the corner of the table before her. Ashby launched at her, pulling her back as the girl took a swipe that missed her by inches.

Red flooded Braith's vision, rage ripped through him. He grabbed hold of the girl, shoving her roughly against the wall. Using Arianna as a shield against Braith's charge, Ashby thrust her before him. His hand wrapped around her throat, pulling her head back as he clamped down on her. A bellow of rage erupted from Braith, he stalked toward Ashby, determined to destroy the man that held the only person Braith cared about anymore.

Ashby didn't make a move to hurt her, but he did keep himself planted firmly behind her. Braith couldn't get at him without having to go through Arianna. Frustration filled him; he could feel the swelling rise of bloodlust tearing through him. "I'm not a fool Braith, I'm not going to kill her unless you force me to," Ashby murmured, barely poking his head out from behind Arianna's back. "I am only looking to talk reasonably, and for you to listen."

Arianna tilted her chin, her eyes blazed with pride, it was apparent that she was irritated at having been snagged and used as a shield. She tried to shrug Ashby's grasp off of her, but he wouldn't let go. "You don't have to manhandle me!" she snapped.

Ashby's hand eased its grip on her throat, for a moment amusement flashed through his bright eyes. However, beneath the amusement, Braith could see his terror. And he had every right to be afraid; Braith was going to kill him for even daring to touch her. "Well aren't you the little spitfire," Ashby whispered.

Arianna turned her head to glare at him, her hands fisted at her sides. "Arianna don't," Braith warned, frightened that she might try something reckless. It's who she was after all. Her enraged, bright eyes came back to him. "Give her back to me and we can talk."

"I know that look in your eyes Braith," Ashby retorted. "I know what you'll do to me if I release her. Just stay calm and everything will be ok."

Braith took another step toward them, Ashby took one back. He pressed against the wall, keeping Arianna before him. "Ashby..."

"I want to walk out of this alive Braith. That is all. I've become content with this simple life; it is not a bad existence. I only wish to keep it."

"If they come here..."

"I don't plan to stay here Braith, I'm not an idiot."

"If that were true then you never would have touched her." Ashby's hand tightened briefly on Arianna, causing her to twitch. "Don't!" Braith snarled.

Ashby's grip eased. "Give me your word that you will not hurt me; that you will let me leave here, alive."

"You have it."

Ashby hesitated, his hand trembled. "I require more than you saying it Braith. Once I release her..."

"Then what do you want?" Braith demanded, panic tearing at his insides. His fingers itched to get a hold of her, to get her away from Ashby's grasp.

"I want *her* word."

"Excuse me?" Braith asked in surprise.

"I won't let Braith hurt you," Arianna breathed. "Is that what you're asking for? Is that what you need to hear?"

Braith balked at such a thought. Arianna held more power over him than anyone he had ever met, but if he was truly set on doing something she couldn't stop him, could she? The thought was ridiculous to him, but even more ridiculous was the stunning realization that it might be true. "You seem like a nice enough girl, I believe you when you say that, but do you really think you could stop him?" Ashby asked.

"I don't understand what you expect from me then," she responded, her annoyance surging to the forefront again.

Ashby poked his head out from around her again; he turned her face toward him. Braith took another step forward, fear pulsed through him. "Don't." He was stricken by the desperation that rattled his voice. If Ashby decided to kill Arianna, she would be dead before Braith could reach them. He was shaken, the monster inside of him was clawing to break free, while the man inside of him was tempted to fall to his knees and beg Ashby to give her back to him, unharmed. He had never been this rattled and terrified before. "Just give her back to me Ashby, I won't hurt you. Just give her back."

Ashby's gaze came back to him. "Is the king's son actually begging? For a girl, for a *human* girl no less?"

He struggled to maintain control. "Why are you taunting him when you know you are going to give me back?" Arianna asked.

"And how do you know that?" Ashby inquired.

"Because you would have killed me already if you weren't, and you said it yourself, all you want from life is fun and pleasure. You may like your women and blood, but you do not like death. And if you kill me your life is over no matter what."

Ashby's finger stroked her face briefly as he studied her. "You are a strange girl," he informed her.

She managed a small smile. "So I've been told."

Ashby actually snorted with laughter. "Oh, I am sure you have."

Though they seemed to be enjoying themselves, Braith was not. "Are you two done!?" he snapped.

"Let me go," Arianna urged him.

Ashby hesitated for a moment, and then he nodded and released her. Braith lurched forward, seizing hold of her as he ripped her away. He realized that he was handling her worse than Ashby had, but he couldn't seem to control himself. He was shaking as he enveloped her. He fought the urge to drag her from here and shelter her from everyone and everything. If it weren't for the fact that he knew they couldn't run forever, he would do just that, but there would be no escape. There would only ever be the fight and misery if things weren't changed; he was beginning to realize that now.

"You can only see around her." Braith lifted his head from Arianna's neck, trying to ignore the powerful beat of her blood as it pumped through her veins, trying to ignore the sweet smell that rose out of her, ensnaring him within its delicious depths. Ashby was watching them in disbelief, his eyes full of amazement. "I didn't see the signs when you first arrived, but I see them now."

"See what signs?" Braith demanded curious as to how Ashby had guessed at the source of his vision. "How do you know anything about what is between us?"

Ashby leaned back in his bonds; his attention turning back to Arianna, there was a gleam of admiration in his bright gaze. "She's your bloodlink."

"She's what?"

Arianna looked completely confused; her eyes stormy and lost. "I thought it was something that only happened between vampires, but apparently I was wrong. I've never heard of it happening with a human before, very strange."

Ashby's voice was filled with awe; he seemed completely astounded by his revelation, whatever that revelation was. Braith was just as lost as Arianna appeared to be. "What are you talking about?" Arianna demanded.

"Well of course you wouldn't know, but Braith..." Ashby's voice trailed off, his eyebrows drew together as his head tilted curiously. "No, you wouldn't know either, would you?"

"Ashby I swear I'll snap your neck just because you're annoying me," Braith was rapidly losing his patience but Ashby was too busy laughing and shaking his head to take Braith's threat as seriously as he should.

"Oh Braith, you are in even worse trouble then I'd suspected. It's not just your family you have to protect her from, it's also *you*."

"What the hell do you mean!?" he all but roared at the infuriating man.

"He means that the royal offspring is royally screwed." Braith froze as the new voice drifted through the house. A voice that was hauntingly familiar.

He held Arianna's head against him as he turned toward the woman standing in the doorway. He hadn't heard her arrive, didn't know how long she had been standing there, or even where she had come from. He cursed himself for such a blunder and blamed his rapidly unraveling control for this mistake. Arianna could have been hurt, she could have been *killed,* and all because he had let his guard down.

His amazement at seeing her appear in the doorway was promptly replaced with his disbelief that she was even here. What was going on? "Melinda."

She smiled, her gaze lingered on Arianna before leisurely turning back to him. "Hello brother."

# CHAPTER FOURTEEN

Aria couldn't help it; she felt her mouth drop in disbelief. Her fingers curled into Braith's hard back. He pulled her toward the main door, the one the woman hadn't appeared in. In fact the strange woman, Braith's *sister*, had appeared thru the door leading to the other rooms. The rooms that Aria knew there was no other entrance into, or at least she'd thought there was no other entrance into them. Apparently she'd been greatly mistaken. Ashby had been a prisoner, of course he would create other escape routes from the tree house. Routes that this woman apparently knew well.

Aria couldn't take her eyes off of the beautiful woman across from them. She was watching her and Braith with rapt attention, her gorgeous gray eyes bright in the glow of the room. Her golden hair tumbled about her shoulders, spilling down her back all the way to her knees. Though she didn't seem to resemble any of her brothers, Melinda did resemble the sister that Aria had met in the palace, Natasha, Ashby's ex-wife.

"I'm not going to harm her Braith."

"What are you doing here Melinda?" Braith spat.

Melinda gradually moved into the room. Her gaze briefly darted to

Ashby. Braith may be confused by his sister's presence here, but Aria knew what had brought her. Or *who*. "Come on Braith, who do you think killed the guards? Who do you think found out the password to relay to the palace? Did you really believe that Ashby was able to do that all by himself?"

"I am very talented," Ashby replied smiling as the beautiful blond stopped beside him.

She quirked a dark eyebrow, her eyes sparkled merrily up at him. "Not that talented love," she assured him.

"Where have you been minx?"

"Well, in case you haven't heard, there's been a huge ado amongst the palace walls. No one seems to know where the eldest prince has gone. Our father is in the process of tearing the town, and the woods apart in search of his missing son. It seems he is blaming the rebels for this affront."

Aria gasped, her hand flew to her mouth as nausea rushed up her throat and she took a hasty step forward. "No," she breathed.

Her friends, her family, they were all being punished because of her and Braith. She didn't want to think about what was being done to them, but she couldn't get her mind off of the consuming knowledge that they were suffering because of her. Braith squeezed her arm but it did nothing to soothe her.

"Well imagine that," Ashby said darkly.

Melinda's smile faded, she caressed Ashby's face. "Did he hurt you?"

Ashby shrugged, but there was nothing carefree about his demeanor now. "Just my pride. You going to untie me?"

Melinda planted her hands on her hips as she surveyed him with interest. "I think I might like you this way."

"You would."

Though Aria was lost in dismay, she could feel the heat creeping rapidly up her face at their words and looks. "Don't," Braith advised when Melinda's fingers dropped to the ropes restraining Ashby.

"Braith," Melinda said plaintively, her demeanor changing rapidly as pure despair shone in her eyes.

"Do *not* untie him Melinda," Braith replied forcefully.

"He won't go after her."

"No, apparently you were always the true traitor amongst us. If you make one more move to untie him, it won't be Arianna that will have to worry about getting hurt."

Ashby straightened, his eyes briefly flashed red as his upper lip curled at the threat. He didn't lunge against the ropes, didn't make a move as he eyed Braith for the first time with true vehemence. Melinda touched Ashby's arm soothingly before folding her hands in front of her. Though she appeared demure, Aria knew that it was only an act. She'd often used the same conduct in the palace, when she was trying to appear far more docile than she was. It hadn't fooled Braith then, it wouldn't fool him now.

"You don't understand," Melinda said pleadingly.

"That you and Ashby conspired to overthrow our father, and blinded me in the process. Yes Melinda, I understand that, even if I don't under-stand the motive behind it."

For the first time Melinda looked truly desperate and frightened as she glanced anxiously at Aria. "If it was her..."

"You don't know her!" Braith snarled.

Melinda tilted her chin up, her jaw clenched as her eyes glimmered with fire. "You're right I don't know her, but I do know that if she was in danger you would do whatever it took to save her."

"Neither of you were ever in peril inside the palace."

"I was married to Natasha, Braith," Ashby reminded him. "We were in danger."

"So you were having an affair and were worried about your lives?" Braith's body was fairly vibrating. Aria tried to ease his betrayal and indignation by stroking his back, but she didn't think there was much she could do in this situation. If it was her, and William or Daniel had betrayed her in such a way, she didn't think she would ever be able to get over it.

"No, there was no affair. From the moment that we met, there was no longer a *Natasha*. There wasn't *any* other woman. It was just us, and if anyone else had known that, if your *family* had known that, they would have done everything they could to destroy what was between us."

Braith appeared doubtful as he raked them both with scathing glances. Melinda's eyes were fervent, desperate as she looked briefly at Aria before focusing her full attention on her brother once more. "Do you really think you could have married Gwendolyn?" she whispered forlornly. "And even if you did manage to force yourself to marry her, do you think you could have lain with her, exchanged blood with her?" At those words her stomach twisted, and Braith looked nearly as repulsed as she felt.

"I didn't think so. If you could, then you would still be in the palace, still be preparing for your wedding. In fact, I've noticed that for the past week you didn't return to your parade of blood slaves, and women. I didn't put two and two together until now, but how was I supposed to know that you had found your escaped little blood slave again, and that you were once again using her to nourish you?"

"I'm not a blood slave!" Aria retorted sharply, growing highly annoyed by the fact that she was still thought of as a piece of property.

Melinda raised a haughty eyebrow at her, but there was a gleam of admiration in her eyes. "She's a feisty one," Ashby murmured approvingly.

Melinda managed a tiny smile as she folded her arms over her chest. "I see that."

"I don't use her," Braith grated.

"You feed from her, do you not?"

"That is not *using* her!" he barked.

Melinda rolled her eyes; she tapped her foot impatiently on the ground. "I understand that she is willing, or I assume she is."

"Of course I am," Aria told her.

"Why?"

"Excuse me?" Aria was startled by the question.

"Why are you willing? You are a human; you are a rebel, why would you give yourself to my brother like that?"

Aria looked up at Braith; she was captivated by his masculine beauty, and the tender soul that he revealed only to her. She thought of him on his knees before her, humbled by her, his heart and soul bared for her to take, or to turn away. She thought of all of his gentleness, the care and protection he had always offered to her, even when he had owned her. He was wonderful, he was everything, and he was hers.

"Because I love him," she whispered. "I always will."

"How sweet," the girl vampire drawled, drawing harsh looks from everyone else in the room. She glowered back at them but wisely remained silent.

Melinda's gray eyes were as cold as steel. "Can you believe it?" Ashby inquired blithely.

"No," Melinda responded.

"I don't care what you believe! It's the truth!" Aria snapped at her.

Melinda's mouth twisted into a smile, Ashby chuckled annoyingly. Aria took a frustrated step forward, but Braith pulled her back. "Stay behind me," he grumbled in warning.

"I believe you love him, I truly do," Melinda pacified. "I just can't believe that it has happened to Braith, of all vampires. Mr. Duty, Mr. Responsibility, Mr. Walk a Straight Line has succumbed to the darkest side of himself."

"Like hell," Braith grated. Aria was surprised to realize that his fangs had extended. His anger and frustration were rapidly unraveling the firm control and restraint he exhibited over himself around others.

Melinda quirked an eyebrow, she shifted a little, her head tipped to the side as she rested a hand on her hip. "Like hell Braith? Like *hell*? Are you forgetting that I live in that damned palace too? Are you forgetting that I was there after she escaped with Jericho? It was a bloodbath Braith; *you* were a one vampire destroyer, one that made even Caleb and father proud. They thought you were finally becoming like them, and in all honesty Braith, so did I. I never suspected that you might actually *care* for the girl. I thought you were reacting in such a way because your pride had been wounded. If I had known the truth, I would have tried to explain it to you, but I don't think you would have listened to me anyway. Especially not while you were immersed in the gluttony of blood and death you had engrossed yourself in."

Aria swallowed heavily, her fingers dug into the rigid muscles cording his arm. He was trembling; his self-loathing evident as he glared at his sister. Melinda painted a vivid picture of what he had been like after she'd fled, and though Aria knew it all, she still hated to hear it.

"I'm not like that," Braith hissed.

"Maybe not normally, and most definitely not before you met her." Melinda took a small step forward, her gaze pinning Braith. Even Aria was surprised by the force of that steely stare. "I'm fairly certain that if I even made one threatening move toward her, you would kill me, sister or not."

Aria waited for Braith to protest that statement; of course he wouldn't kill his own sister. She found herself waiting until she finally had to turn her attention back to him. "Braith?" She finally inquired, stunned by the fact that he hadn't responded yet.

He seemed hesitant to answer, and when he did, he didn't sound all that convincing. "I wouldn't kill you."

"You would if you had to. You would if it became necessary to ensure her survival."

"No, he wouldn't," Aria insisted.

"Is that true Braith, you wouldn't?" Melinda demanded. "Are you going to stand here and lie in front of her, *to* her?"

Aria's heart pumped laboriously. Her soul ached for him, for herself, for the sister staring so forcefully at her brother. "I won't lie to her," Braith grated. "Yes, I would kill you if it meant her life."

Aria inhaled sharply, she could barely breathe through the disbelief rocking her. "Braith?"

"Don't be so appalled," Melinda told her. "I would try to kill him too, if it came to Ashby. We can't help it, you are his bloodlink; Ashby is mine. We don't have a choice, if you were a vampire you would under-stand the driving force that propels us to make sure that they are safe, and kept with us. You would also understand the fact that your humanity tests every boundary of his control. I saw what happened in that palace, what he did. You were still alive then, if you were to die..." Her eyes grew briefly distant, she shuddered. "If you were to die then it would be as if hell itself had unleashed its wrath upon this earth. No one would be safe."

Braith was trembling with barely leashed power. Aria rubbed his arm lightly, trying to calm him, but she wasn't getting through. It wasn't his sister's words so much that were upsetting him; it was the fact that she had mentioned Aria's death. "Braith..."

"She's not going to die," he said simply, lost to the haze of emotions clouding him.

"Not for a long time," Aria assured him.

"*Ever.*"

The room was silent, staggered by the low spoken word. Aria's heart hammered, she knew that he would like her to change, but to do so... To do so would be to become everything she had ever hated and fought against. To do so would be to turn against her own kind, her own family. Her chest was tight, tears burned her eyes.

"Braith," she breathed.

He turned toward her, his arm was shaking even more; the muscles within it were trembling in her grasp. "You know how dangerous that is," Ashby said.

Aria was fairly certain that Braith hadn't heard him though. His attention was focused upon her, his entire being was connected to hers, linked with hers. She could become a vampire and stay with her family; they would forgive her eventually, maybe. She would also be a strong ally for them; Braith would be a powerhouse on their side. She could become a vampire and stay with him forever. She could give him this, if it was what he so desperately needed. She could give him this, because he would give her anything that he could.

He had not chosen whatever was happening to him, to *them*. Braith prided himself on control, on stability, and self reliance. He prided himself on the fact that he was powerful, yet understanding. Since she'd left the palace though, he'd been none of those things. He had become angry, unstable, and the murderous monster he despised his father and brother for. Melinda and Ashby understood what was going on, and perhaps if Braith did he would be a little more stable, but right now his confusion over his wild emotions was only adding to his volatility.

"Arianna?" his voice, so deep and beautiful was ragged with feeling.

"It will be fine," she promised fervently. His eyes, fevered and desperate, softened. In their bright depths she saw his confusion, but she also saw his craving; his *love*. "We can do this, we can do anything."

"It's not that simple," Ashby interjected. "Braith knows that. You aren't a vampire, that's why I am so surprised this has happened between you. It's never happened with a human before, never."

"I think you have to tell me exactly what is happening here," Braith said coldly.

"Can I untie him first?" Melinda inquired.

"No."

Annoyance flared through her steely gaze, her hands fisted at her sides in futility. They may be siblings, but it wouldn't be an equal fight. Braith was older, stronger; he radiated a depth of power that Melinda didn't seem to possess. "Imagine if it was her that was tied up; imagine how you would feel then Braith!" she pleaded.

"It's not her, and it never will be."

"Braith!" Melinda's frustration was mounting; her eyes were growing darker, redder. Her emotions were wildly swinging toward the breaking point.

"Easy love," Ashby comforted. "It's ok, I'm fine. Braith doesn't know how to tie someone up all that well anyway." His eyes were gleaming with amusement, but Aria could sense the tension beneath his blithe façade. The last thing he wanted was to see Melinda try and fight her way through her brother.

Melinda remained wary; she leaned over and placed a quick kiss upon Ashby's mouth. Aria pitied them; she couldn't imagine being kept from Braith in such a way. Yet there were two of them, separately they weren't much of a threat to Braith, together they could be.

"Let your brother know what is going on, maybe then he won't look like he's about to go on a rampage and slaughter us all," Ashby urged.

Aria stepped closer to Braith; she needed to feel and touch more of him. She had a feeling she wasn't going to like what Melinda and Ashby had to tell them. He wrapped his arm around her waist. His body was cooler than hers, but heat still flooded through her as her chest was brought up flush against his side. His hand briefly stroked over her, his eyes burned into hers.

"Have you ever heard the term bloodlink?" Melinda inquired, breaking into their moment.

Braith reluctantly turned away from her. "No, I haven't."

"Neither had I, until I met Ashby." Her gaze traveled leisurely to him, she reached out a delicate hand and clasped hold of his outstretched one. They seemed to take solace from the feel of one another as their hands entwined. "And then the whole world was completely right, and so completely wrong."

"I was already married to Natasha," Ashby continued.

Melinda's face scrunched up, disgust flitted over her delicate features. "If you recall, I was with mother when their wedding occurred. I was too young to stay behind when father banished her and he didn't want the responsibility of taking care of me. It wasn't until she was killed that I was allowed back into the palace."

"I had been married to Natasha for five years at that point," Ashby said.

"I remember," Braith interjected coldly.

Ashby grinned at him. "We used to have fun in those days. Before the war, when everything was still easy. You were the reigning heir and I was a vampire with a title, money, women, and a wife that cared as little for me as I did for her. Ok, well the wife part may have sucked, but mostly we avoided each other. All we had to do was conceive a son in order to make your father happy, and then we wouldn't have to be with each other again. It just wasn't working for us."

Melinda's eyes had grown darker at the mention of her sister; her face was as stormy as a tumultuous sky. Ashby brought Melinda's hand to his mouth, kissing her as he sought to ease her tension. "Then mom was killed, the war broke out, and I was sent back to the palace," Melinda said tersely.

"Your father was always greedy, always aspired to have more. He just never banked on so many vampires being *content* with their way of life. He never even considered the fact that some of the other powerful families might not go along with him. And he never expected that I planned to get out of my marriage from one sister, because I had lost my soul to the other one."

They seemed to silently communicate with each other before Ashby turned his attention back to them. "A bloodlink is something that happens between vampires, and apparently with humans also. It happened to my parents; that is how I knew about it, and what the signs of it were. Most vampires believe it is a myth because it is so rare, but I knew that it was true, I just never thought it would happen to me. My parents were fortunate enough to find each other and not have any obstacles in their way. Unfortunately we weren't, and neither are you.

"My parents saw the war as a chance to escape the tyrannical rule of your father; I saw it as a chance to break free of my wife. It was a chance to start anew and build a better life with Melinda, so I took it. You were caught in the crossfire Braith, but I really didn't mean for you to get hurt. As retribution for our mutiny my family was killed, but your father thought this was a better punishment for me."

"Thankfully," Melinda breathed.

"What exactly is a bloodlink?" Aria inquired.

"It's a deep connection between vampires. Our blood calls to each other. We grow stronger off of it when we share it. The connection is instantaneous, as Braith well knows, and it is unbreakable. It will eat you alive if you're kept from each other, something else that Braith seems to have discovered."

"Stronger from it," Aria mulled.

"Of course dear," Ashby purred. "It's why Braith can see again, but I'm guessing it's only when you are near."

"What?" Melinda gasped. "Braith?"

Braith was silent for a moment; the tension in him was growing by the second. "Yes, I can see when she is near. What about the two of you?"

Aria swallowed nervously. Braith could see, and it was a miracle, but could they also perform miracles? Had she completely misjudged this situation, was Braith weaker than them? She glanced between Melinda and Ashby, and then turned back at Braith. No, it was obvious who the strongest was, but if Ashby were to get free...

Melinda was frowning fiercely. "Ashby..."

"I know love."

"Melinda, you may be my sister but if you don't tell me I will destroy him," Braith told her.

Aria shuddered, her hands tightened on Braith's arm. She wanted to promise that she would never let that happen, the last thing she wanted was to ruin their love, but if there was any chance they might attack Braith, she wasn't going to say anything. It was better that they were afraid of Braith for now. Melinda took a protective step closer to Ashby.

"We don't have anything like that Braith. We're stronger because we have each other; we're stronger because the bond between us has made us stronger. We feed off of each other, which is something that most vampires will not allow to happen, our blood helps to enhance our power and speed. As a united front we will prevail over a lone vampire, and death is the only thing that will divide us. But you..."

"You are different," Ashby finished for her. "Maybe because she is human, maybe because you are the prince apparent, the first born, and your blood is more powerful than your siblings, but you've had a stronger reaction to the link than any I've ever heard of."

"You've actually had a *physical* strengthening reaction without the blood," Melinda continued. "I'm assuming that is why you bought her in the first place, because you actually saw her then."

Braith gave a crisp nod of confirmation. "Imagine if she becomes a vampire?" Ashby pondered.

"Is it possible?" Melinda wondered.

Aria frowned at the two of them. "I don't know," Ashby admitted. "But I think they have more than a bloodlink. I think they may have an even stronger bond."

"You may be right," Melinda agreed. "For him to get his eyesight back like that is so strange."

"It is," Ashby confirmed.

Aria sensed Braith's mounting aggravation and she was growing just as frustrated by the couple as he was. "Enough!" he snapped, causing Melinda to jump slightly. "Enough, the both of you, *enough*. If you are so close, then why is there another vampire here?"

They both frowned in confusion then their gaze drifted to the girl who had stayed utterly silent, though she was listening raptly to them. "Oh her," Melinda replied, giggling softly. Ashby brought her hand up to his chest, enfolding it within his. Braith's composure was rapidly unraveling. They didn't know what they were messing with right now, didn't know that he was close to losing all control. Aria knew though. She had seen him in the woods with those vampires. She had seen what he was capable of, the punishment and death he could deal out so swiftly and without remorse.

"Melinda," Aria prodded.

The smile slipped from Melinda as she finally focused on Braith again. "She's just a girl from town; they knew that I would be coming back soon."

"How?" Braith growled. "And why would she come here?"

"I manage to sneak out of the palace more often than you know. As the youngest and most ineffective child, no one ever pays attention to my comings and goings. I bring blood slaves here with me when I can, in order to keep the people in the area quiet about the fact that there are no guards anymore. She is here in the hopes of returning to town with whatever I might have managed to smuggle out."

"Why?" Braith demanded.

"To keep Ashby safe of course. I killed the guards years ago, but Ashby couldn't escape. There was nowhere for us to go. Every village knows who Ashby is, father made certain of that, and the reward for him is large enough for any starving vamp to hand Ashby over, no matter how much they may hate father. But only one person, or one family, could get that reward, not the entire village. And no matter what, there was no guarantee that father would actually give them the money. I bought the loyalty of the people closest to here by promising them a steady supply of blood, if they kept their mouths shut. It was more than father could promise all of them."

Aria bowed her head beneath the implication of those words, nausea twisted through her. She was certain she was going to be sick. Her people had been used to buy silence; their lives had been freely traded away as if they meant nothing. "Awful," she breathed.

"Life is not always roses and sunshine dear." A chill crept down Aria's spine, she found herself unable to hold Melinda's cold gaze. "And I would do anything to keep Ashby alive, just as I am assuming you would do the same for Braith."

Aria bit on her bottom lip, she couldn't look at any of them. She would do anything for Braith, but to freely trade lives for his, she didn't think she could do that. But then, she was human, and they were not. They thought little of her species; humans were beneath them, they didn't care what happened to them. Aria knew she would freely trade a vampire life for his, she was certain of that.

"There are things that have to be done in order to secure the bond between bloodlinks," Ashby explained.

Braith squeezed her hand. He was trying to comfort her, but Aria could not shake the dread rolling through her. This was not her world, she didn't belong in this place of blood and death and strange bloodlinks that allowed the blind to see. What was she doing here? How did she get involved in all of this?

But the answer to those questions was standing before her, willing to die for her, as he used his body to block her from whatever attack might come their way. Her heart swelled, tears burned her eyes. She didn't fit in this world, but she realized now that she would never be leaving it again. She hadn't realized it at the time, but when she'd chosen to leave the woods with Braith, she had sealed her fate. There was no turning back, and even though she was frightened by the uncertainty of their future, she was willing to endure the challenges that were still to come.

"And those are?" Braith inquired.

"Exchange of blood, sex," Ashby continued. Aria's face burned, it was all she could do to keep standing before them. "But those are vampire interactions. With this, I'm assuming that the change will also be necessary."

"And if she doesn't survive it?" Melinda asked.

"Then I doubt any of us will," Ashby muttered.

Aria finally managed to lift her head to stare at them. "I'm not going to die," she told them.

Ashby and Melinda leveled her with identical looks of hopelessness. "Most do not survive the change. The human body is too frail; it simply cannot take it. If you stay human it is certain that one day you will die. And Braith will go crazy from it."

"And that's only if you are willing to become a vampire," Melinda elaborated.

Braith turned toward her, she could feel the full force of his gaze upon her, but she couldn't find the words to answer his unspoken question. Was she willing to become a vampire? Was she willing to live in that world? Was she willing to *die*? Willing to drink blood and feed from her people? She lifted her gaze to Braith's, she could feel the tears burning in her eyes, but they did not slip free. He was so strong, so powerful, and wise. He was ancient compared to her, a near god in his world. She was a fighter, and she was strong, but he could snap her bones with a flick of his wrist. And yet, as he looked upon her, she could see the vulnerability in his gaze, the uncertainty that blazed from him and made him almost as weak as she was.

She did that to him, she *was* doing it to him, and she hated herself for it. Her fingers brushed against his face, she loved the feel of his hardness and stubble beneath her hand. He awed her, and inspired her in so many ways. "You humble me also," she whispered.

A low groan escaped him; he lifted her as if she weighed no more than a feather and pressed her against him. His hands were in her hair, his lips against her cheek and ear. "It will not be so Arianna," he whispered. She pulled back to stare at him questioningly. "I will not take the risk of killing you. I will not *be* the one that kills you."

Aria frowned at him; she bent her forehead to his. "I *will* survive it."

"There is no guarantee. I will not risk it."

"But I will die no matter what!"

He managed a halfhearted smile. "Then I will just have to make sure it is not for a *very* long time."

"I will grow old."

"You will grow even more beautiful. And when you are gone, I will follow you."

Tears spilled down her cheeks. She was far more accepting of her own death than she was of his. But then again, she had expected to die every day since she was old enough to realize what death was. "No Braith. No. I see the way you are now, what you said earlier, in the kitchen..."

"I was wrong," he said firmly. "It was a moment of weakness, it won't happen again. I will *not* do that to you."

His eyes were beautiful, bright as he watched her, smiled at her, and loved her. He kissed her lightly, his mouth warm and pliant against her own. For a moment Aria allowed herself to forget there were other people in the room and there was only the two of them. For a small fraction of a second, there was total joy, total happiness, and true awe in a world that often lacked such things.

Then Braith was pulling away and the world was once again

intruding upon them. Aria wrapped her arms around his neck. She dropped her head to his shoulder and buried her face in his neck, trying to keep the world at bay for a little longer. He continued to hold her firmly, but she knew his attention was not solely focused upon her anymore. As prince, as the future ruler of his world, and hers, he had other matters to attend to.

# CHAPTER FIFTEEN

Arianna was finally asleep, but it had only been a matter of time before exhaustion won out over her stubborn nature. She'd fought against it for awhile but had finally succumbed to the requirements of her body. She was curled up on the couch, her head in his lap, her hand curled around his thigh.

He trailed his hand across her silken hair, letting it slide through his fingers. Melinda was watching him with interest, but she didn't protest the fact that Braith still refused to untie Ashby. She may be his sister, but he was not going to be outnumbered by them. Not when Arianna's life was on the line.

Though there was tension in Ashby's eyes, his posture remained casual, and he retained his mischievous air as Melinda leaned against him. "I never suspected anything between you two," Braith muttered.

"There was a lot going on at the time." Melinda's gaze drifted toward Arianna. "I never suspected anything between the two of *you* either, but then I never thought you were capable of love. Especially not with a human, and especially not with your blood slave, though I was curious as to why you had finally taken one. Now I know why."

Braith didn't take offense to her words. He hadn't thought he was capable of love either. He cared for his brother Jericho; he even cared for Melinda, though he had never known her as well as Caleb or Natasha. Even when Melinda had returned to the palace, she had remained mostly distant from her other siblings. However, she hadn't really known them as she'd spent her first twenty seven out of thirty years in exile, with their mother.

The war had been raging in full force by the time Melinda returned, Braith had only seen her a handful of times before his vision was lost. Though she had continued to mature over time, most of her growing had been completed before he was blinded; she hadn't changed much since then. Even after he'd lost his vision, he'd only come into contact with her once a month, if even. He'd assumed that she did the same things as Natasha. That she drifted about the palace, enjoying the luxuries, and thriving on the blood.

Apparently she had actually been escaping into the wilderness to nourish and spend time with her lover. Melinda had always seemed so sweet and young to him. Apparently her picturesque face, and serene demeanor, hid a far stronger personality than he had ever suspected.

"Why did you keep returning to the palace? Why didn't you just stay here?"

"Someone had to bring back the slaves and keep the locals around here quiet. Someone had to make sure they didn't send out new guards, and if they did, we had to be prepared to take care of them. Someone had to spy, to see if there would ever be a chance that we could escape together, and finally be free."

Braith nodded, impressed by his sisters cunning, daring, and skill. He was also put off by her manipulation and cold admission about her deceptions. He made a mental note not to trust her, he didn't think she was inherently cruel, but it was more than obvious she would do anything to keep Ashby safe, and Braith was certain that Ashby would do the same thing for her. Neither of them was going to leave his sight until Jack arrived. It was the only way he would feel marginally better about Arianna's safety.

Arianna stirred, her hand constricted on his thigh. "You know that you don't have a prayer of keeping her human," Ashby told him.

"I won't change her."

"You may not *want* to change her, you may think that you can keep yourself from doing so, but we all know the truth here Braith. You think you can go the next five, ten, *fifty* years risking her life, and watching her die?"

"If I have to."

Ashby shook his head; he leaned back against the wall. The young vampire girl remained silent; she'd offered no further protests to her restraints. She was sullen, resigned to remaining tied up for now. "You're only in the beginning stages of this Braith." Ashby folded his hands before him as he stared unflinchingly at Braith. "Do you think it's going to get *easier* as the years go on? It grows and intensifies; the bond between you will become something so intense that it will take every-thing you have to get through one *second* without her. You asked me earlier who I was expecting; do you think it was *this* girl?" He gestured sharply at the young vampire girl.

"No, I thought it was Melinda at the door. Do you know how difficult it is to see her go back there? I hate myself *every* time she leaves here, *every* time she returns to that depraved shit hole. If there was ever a time she didn't return from the palace, I would be there in a heartbeat, killing everyone in my way until they finally took me down. I would welcome the death they would finally deliver to me. She's *human* Braith; you will live with her mortality every second of your life together. You won't be able to handle it, I can promise you that."

Braith glowered at him. "I'm stronger than you."

Ashby snorted as he sat back. "Bull. You're physically stronger than all of us, but you are by far the weakest amongst us right now. Your Achilles heel is lying on your lap, and if any of your enemies get a hold of her, they will control you completely. If they kill her, you are done for. Smarten up Braith. Yes, you are stronger with her in your life, but you are also far weaker. Especially if she stays human."

"I don't have much of a choice on that front."

"Keep her human until you figure out what you mean to do. Though, I'm beginning to suspect that might be taking your father down, am I right?"

Melinda's eyes widened, her delicate mouth parted. "No," she breathed.

Ashby squeezed her hand as his bright eyes gleamed eagerly. "Yes love, I believe that Braith has finally realized that there is something more important than duty, honor, and obedience. Right?"

"I will not kill my father," he grated.

"No, I'm not even sure you could, but you *do* have the advantage of sight again, and I'm assuming he doesn't know that."

"He doesn't," Melinda confirmed when Braith didn't.

Ashby nodded, his fingers twirled idly, Braith could almost see the gears churning within his devious mind. "You wouldn't kill Caleb either. But if you *could* take them down, overthrow their rule, wrest control from them, you would. *If* you can get enough help to do it. It's why you came here."

Braith had forgotten how perceptive Ashby was. It was annoying the hell out of him right now. "You're hoping that I may still have ties to the rebellious families that fought with mine, and somehow managed to avoid capture. You're hoping that I may still know some vampires that might be willing to help you, and the only reason you would like to know those things was if you intended to oust the king. Am I wrong Braith?"

Braith turned his attention to the window. He wouldn't deny Ashby's words, nor would he confirm them. He hadn't left the palace with the objective of ousting his father from power. He hadn't gone after Arianna in those caverns because he had decided that he was going to fight, he hadn't pulled her free of there with the intention of one day claiming the throne (he still wasn't sure he would do that, it depended on Arianna). He had just planned to get her somewhere safe, get her to people that might be able to shelter her, and to try and live a peaceful life with her.

Somewhere along the way though, he had realized that there was nowhere safe for her, and no one that could protect her, except for him. And if he was going to keep her safe, then his father would have to be removed. A new power, and a new world system, would have to be established.

"This will be interesting, a civil war," Ashby pondered. "A civil war involving the most powerful regime to ever rule us, a war between the murderous, vicious father, and the son who hates him; imagine the conse-quences of such a thing, imagine the horror."

Braith stiffened as he turned back to them. Relief radiated from

Melinda, hope gleaming in her eyes. "Or imagine the wonder of it," she whispered. "Imagine the freedom that would come if such a tyrannical, ruthless ruler could be broken."

"Is it your love for Ashby that has so turned you against our father?" Braith inquired.

She tilted her head as she quirked a dark eyebrow at him. In that moment it struck him how very much she looked like their mother. He had never thought much of it; he hadn't really thought much of his mother, as he had been taken from her at a young age. His father hadn't allowed him to spend too much time with a woman he was worried might coddle Braith, and weaken him. The same thing had happened with Caleb and Jericho. He wasn't sure when Natasha had been taken away, and Melinda had still been a toddler when their mother was banished from the castle. The king had cared nothing for the youngest child that had left with the woman.

"No Braith, that isn't the reason. I have always hated him."

"I didn't realize that."

"You wouldn't." Braith stared ferociously at her for a moment, but Melinda didn't back down from him. "You were in your own world Braith. You were the prince, the future king; you thought nothing of the young sister who suddenly reappeared in your home. And once you lost your vision I was even further from your mind, from everyone's mind. No one noticed when I disappeared for a day or two, sometimes even a week at a time. I am a nonentity in that place, I always have been, and that is just fine by me.

"You had it far worse than I ever did, even with my early years outside of the palace walls. I understood my circumstances were better than the scrutiny, and constant cloud of hatred and disappointment you had to live under. You were never going to be the monster that father tried to make you. No matter how badly he treated you, no matter how often he beat you. Caleb should have been the first born son. He's the only one father even remotely approved of."

"It would have made things easier, and father happier," Braith agreed without sorrow.

"Caleb may be harder to overthrow than father. If he hasn't already realized it, he soon will know that he is the new heir apparent. He won't give that up easily, and the things he will do with that power..."

Melinda shuddered; her hand tightened on Ashby's, who looked just as appalled as Melinda. Even the vampire girl was watching them with protruding, frantic eyes. What Caleb would do with that power would make everything his father had done seem petty and small. Blood would spill freely through the palace streets. Debauchery and death would rule.

"How were you able to survive the day that mother was killed?" Braith inquired. He had never asked before, never even thought to, or even given much thought to the fact that his sister had survived the fight that had claimed their mother.

Melinda closed her eyes, her hands fisted in her lap. Pain flickered briefly across her features as her lip trembled. Ashby rested his hand on her shoulder, squeezing it reassuringly. "Isn't that obvious?" Braith tensed, he hadn't realized that Arianna had awakened until she spoke. Her eyes were slightly swollen with sleep, but they were dark and swirling with pain as she sat up. Her question hung in the air; she waited expectantly for him to say something.

"No," he admitted, feeling as if he were somehow disappointing her by not knowing the answer.

Her eyes were filled with sadness as she rested her small hand upon his face. However, the sorrow was not for her, or even for Melinda, it was for *him*. Braith was stunned by the grief he saw there, he didn't understand it. "Your mother sacrificed herself for Melinda."

Braith started, he frowned at Arianna as he seized hold of her hand and pulled it away from his cheek. "How could you possibly know that?" he demanded.

Her full mouth was tremulous, tears burned in her beautiful sapphire eyes. "Because it's how William and I survived."

Braith was taken aback. He turned toward Melinda, surprised to find his sister watching Arianna with compassion. "Is that true?" he demanded. "Did our mother sacrifice herself for you?"

"Yes," Melinda confirmed.

Braith slowly digested this information. He hadn't really known his mother; she'd been kind to him during their brief time together, but he hadn't known what life had been like for her within the palace, or outside of it.

"Why would she do that?"

It was not Melinda that answered, but Arianna. "Love. Simple, unconditional love."

He watched Arianna, saw the need in her eyes, the burning desire for him to understand. And he *did* understand. He understood the kind of love that she was talking about, what it was to die for someone else, because he would die for her. A few months ago, before he had met her, he never would have fathomed doing such a thing for someone else. Now there was nothing that could stop him from saving her life.

"I understand," he assured her. Her smile was tremulous, a single tear slipped free. He wiped it gently away. "What happened?"

Arianna shied away from him, her eyes darkened, darted away, and then slid back to him. Her jaw clenched, her chin jutted proudly out. "Our father thought it would be best to hide us, not in the forest, but in a home. He felt if we were out of the woods, if we were living an almost normal life we would be safe, and we would blend in. We lived there for about a year, and then one day the troops came to raid the village.

"My father had built a small room for all of us to hide in just in case that ever happened. It was a panic room of sorts, there was food, air, water to survive for days. We could have stayed in there until the soldiers left, until my father came back. We could have *all* stayed in that room." Arianna's dark eyebrows drew together sharply. Her lips were pursed; the awfulness of the memory was etched onto her features and beautiful eyes.

"But you didn't?"

She focused on him, blinking as she seemed to come back to the present. "No, we didn't." Her tone was clipped, harsh, her voice ragged.

"Why?"

She licked her lips, her forehead furrowed; she appeared confused by this question. "I didn't understand that at the time either. She put William and I in that room, told us to remain silent no matter what happened, no matter what we heard, and then she closed the door."

Braith took hold of her hand as she shuddered. "And what did you do?"

She looked helplessly at him. "Nothing, we did nothing. There was nothing that we could do. We were four years old, we were terrified, and we didn't know how to get out of that room. We tried, but we couldn't find the way out, and then they came into that house. We sat in a corner, and we held each other, and we cried. We did what our mother told us to do, and we listened in silence as they tortured and killed her. The entire time she swore that we had gone out with our father, that we were not present."

He didn't think she was aware of the tears sliding down her cheeks. He didn't think she was aware of anything outside of the past that she seemed to be trapped within. A past he would have done anything to take from her, but there was nothing that he could do. There was no way to right her past, no way to ease her sorrow; all he could do was give her a better future.

He pulled her close, rubbing the nape of her neck as he tenderly kissed her forehead. She grasped each of his forearms, clinging to him as if he were a life raft in the sea of her agony. "There was nothing else you could have done," he assured her.

A small smile curved Arianna's mouth, but there was no humor in it. "That may be true, but I'll never believe it."

He closed his eyes, savoring in the amazing scent of her. She engulfed him, filled him, she eased every awful thing inside of him. He trusted that he did the same for her. "Why didn't she go in the room?" Ashby asked.

"Because the soldiers would have torn the house apart looking for the three of them so she sacrificed herself, she allowed them to torture her until they were satisfied that her children really weren't there. Right?" Melinda inquired.

Arianna nodded. "Yes. I believe that is why."

Braith thought about the woman that had given life to Arianna, the one that had helped create it, and in the end saved it. He gave a silent thanks to her; he guessed that the proud, brave, giving, and strong person before him was exactly as her mother had been.

"Is that what your mother did?" Arianna asked.

"I was older, not quite a child anymore, barely a teen when they came," Melinda confirmed. "My mother managed to get us upstairs before they invaded our house. She pulled us into one of the backrooms, and using furniture she blocked the door to the best of her ability. She helped me out the window, pushing me down the small roof before helping me slip over the side. She promised me that she would follow before I dropped to the ground. Instead, she scurried back up the roof, slid the window shut, and locked it. By then I could hear them breaking down the door and shoving the furniture aside to get at her. She fought them off in order to buy me more time to escape.

"I tried to go back in after her. But I was stopped by four of the servants we had. Mother had always been good to them; she had always treated them with respect and kindness. She had taught me to do the same, and over the years we became more like a family. I was young, and though they were not strong vampires, the four of them overwhelmed me. They forced me away from that awful place. One of them went back the next day for mother's body.

"We buried her in the woods beneath her favorite willow, and marked her grave with a simple stone."

Arianna rubbed her thumbs leisurely over his hand. He was sorry that Melinda had suffered through such a loss; sorry she'd had to witness it. He hated the fact that his mother had been killed, that she'd known only terror at the end. But there was something else that Melinda said that had ensnared his attention.

"You didn't come back to the palace until you were in your twenties."

Melinda frowned at him. "I know."

"Then you weren't a young teen when she died."

"I was fourteen when she was killed Braith."

A strange tension was growing inside of him. He had never asked Melinda her story, had never thought much about it. Their mother, a woman he had barely seen in the eight hundred years before her death, hadn't meant much to him. But, she had still been his mother, and Melinda was still his sister. He required answers.

"Where were you all those years Melinda?" he grated out. Arianna shifted nervously, she sensed his escalating tension and ire.

Melinda swallowed nervously, Ashby patted her hand reassuringly. "It's ok Melinda, tell him."

"Tell me what?" When she continued to stay silent, he rose to his feet. "Tell me what?" he grated.

"Braith, give her time," Arianna urged.

"Were you with the rebels? Did they capture you after you buried her?" he demanded.

"The rebels?" Melinda inquired her confusion evident.

"The rebels that killed her," he snarled impatiently.

Melinda bit on her lip, Arianna rose to her feet beside him. He could hear the furious beat of her heart; she was already looking at him with concern. Her hand began to tremble within his. "I never said that she was killed by rebels Braith," Melinda whispered.

Something stirred at the far edges of his mind; something dark and sinister began to make its way through him. Braith straightened his shoulders, taking strength in Arianna's presence at his side. "Then who?" he demanded.

Melinda's lip was trembling. Ashby had risen to his feet, he stepped forward, placing his body in front of Melinda's, but Braith had no intention of going after his sister. It was the last thing in the world that he was going to do. "They were father's men Braith. It was father's guards that came into that house. It was *father* that had her killed. I didn't return to the palace until I was accidentally discovered ten years later. I never planned to return, I hated the man, and I was certain he would kill me too."

Braith was frozen, he couldn't move through the outrage that gripped him. "Where were you all that time?" Arianna wondered.

"Hiding with our servants. It was dumb luck that I was caught, that I was forced back there. They had presumed me dead, though the guards had been honest with father and told him that they had not seen me. They assumed that I had either died before the raid, or that I had been somewhere else and died later; they felt it unlikely that I was able to survive and stay hidden on my own. I was in a village that had been deemed a possible traitorous threat when it was raided, my servants, my *family* was killed. If Jericho hadn't been with them I probably would have been killed also, but even after all our years apart, he recognized me."

"Blood knows blood," Braith said. Arianna shuddered.

"He's the reason I'm still alive."

"Does he know what happened to our mother?"

Melinda swallowed heavily, Ashby was becoming edgier. "I hid it from him at first, but when he wanted to bring me back to the palace I refused to go. I was afraid of father, of what he would do to me. I became hysterical when he insisted that I was to return, when he tried to force me back I spilled the story and told him why I couldn't return. He is the only other one that knows the truth.

"He told me to tell father that I had seen nothing the day our mother was killed; that the servants had taken me out shopping that day, and only found mother's body that night. I was to tell him that I hadn't returned to the palace because I was uncertain of how to get there, and fearful of wandering too far from the only home I'd ever known. He told me not to say anything, but that he *had* to take me back. The other guards had seen me; there was no way that he could let me go without looking suspicious. Father would continue to hunt me until I was uncovered again, and he would probably kill me when he did find me. But if I went back on my own I would be able to keep my knowledge of events to myself. No matter how outraged and resentful I was, I had no choice but to return. All I could do was hope to escape one day."

"Jack knew about this," Braith grated. "The whole time."

"Jack?" Ashby asked in surprise.

"Jericho," Arianna answered when Braith remained silent. He was furious that his father had done this and that his siblings had kept him in the dark, *furious* that he had stood by his father's side, and been a pawn in all of their lies and deceit. He understood their reasons why they hadn't told him, but he would like to throttle them all for their duplicity. It wouldn't continue. He may not be his father's heir anymore, but he was still a prince, he was still *the* next in line. He would set right all of the wrongs that he had so blindly followed. "When Jericho came to live with us in the forest, he changed his name to Jack. It's what we know him as."

"It's *who* he is," Braith grated. Arianna glanced up at him in surprise, her hands were firm in his grasp, warm, and oh so very fragile. "It's who he's been since he encountered Melinda. It was only six years ago that he was able to break free and officially become Jack and allow that other side of him to come out. He left the palace with no intention of ever returning to it."

The betrayal was sharp, and far deeper than he had expected it to be. When Jack had taken Arianna, Braith had known that Jack had changed, that he was not the brother he had always known, but Jack hadn't been that brother for *far* longer than Braith had ever suspected. Arianna leaned against him; she released his hand to wrap her arm around his waist, holding him closer to her. Her forehead rested against his chest, he could feel her distress and knew that it was for him.

"Why didn't you tell me?" he demanded.

"Because we were trying to keep you safe. No matter how little you knew our mother, your sense of duty, your sense of responsibility, your sense of *honor* would have driven you to go after father, and he *would* have killed you. We decided to wait, to bide our time until we thought that there might actually be a chance to take father down."

"And you believe that time is now?"

Melinda's gray eyes flickered, sadness crept into them. "If you had asked me that five months ago I would have said no, but I hadn't known that Jericho had immersed himself in the resistance until he took her, and I never would have guessed that you would decide to relinquish your title for a human. You are a powerful ally Braith, the rebels are powerful allies, and I believe that even if we weren't expecting it that yes, this is the time. Things are rapidly changing and I don't think there is any way to change the flow of *this* tide. Not anymore."

"Were you ever going to tell me?"

"One day. We weren't entirely sure when, we were just waiting for the right moment. I never expected you to fall in love with a human, your *blood* slave, and to have her be one of the prominent figures of the resistance no less. How could anyone have seen *that* coming?"

Braith took strength in Arianna's presence, and unwavering love and loyalty, but it couldn't ease the betrayal festering inside of him. He had thought that Caleb and Natasha were the deceitful and manipulative ones, apparently he was wrong. It seemed they were all dark and twisted in their own ways; they had all held and kept their secrets from each other.

"What a trusting family we are," he drawled sarcastically.

"We were only trying to keep everyone as safe as possible," Melinda said. "If father had known anything..." Her voice trailed off, horror filled her gaze as she shook her head. "Awful, it would have been awful."

Braith silently agreed, but he wasn't willing to concede anything to her. "Your father used the war as an excuse to kill your mother, and probably Melinda, but why?" Arianna questioned.

"Because he didn't use the war as an excuse to kill our mother, he used it as an excuse to *start* the war." Arianna jumped in surprise, but Braith had sensed Jack's steady approach a few minutes ago.

Braith smoothly pushed Arianna toward the wall as he turned to face his brother. He couldn't stop his instinctual urge to protect her from the people that had entered the room. Even before she uttered the word dad, he knew immediately which one of the seasoned, disbelieving, infuriated men was her father.

And that man was mad enough to kill.

# CHAPTER SIXTEEN

ARIA TRIED to take a step toward her father, but Braith held her back. The muscles in his ridged arms clamped against her, the taut muscles of his body rippled beneath his clothes. She hadn't missed the fact that Braith had turned her, putting her in a more secure position, using his body to defend hers.

There was no reason for him to protect her though. This was her father, her family. As she watched William and Daniel slipped into the room behind Jack and her father. "It's ok Braith," she whispered.

"Wait," he hissed; his voice low and commanding. She frowned at him, but didn't fight against his hold. He was thrown off balance right now; he needed her with him in order to keep himself steady. Otherwise he might injure someone in this room, someone she cared about, someone *he* cared about.

"You told him everything?" Jack inquired.

Melinda nodded; she stepped closer to Ashby as she eyed Aria's family warily. Melinda didn't trust her own kind, and it was more than apparent she didn't trust humans either. Especially *rebel* humans. "Can I untie him now?" she asked of Braith, her voice wavering slightly. He remained unmoving, his eyes dark and intense. "We can't take you down Braith; all of us combined probably couldn't take you down."

"He knows that, and that's not what he's worried about. That's *never* what he's worried about anymore," Jack responded.

"Then what!?" Melinda demanded, her composure beginning to unravel. She was so frustrated with him, incensed that Ashby was still being restrained. "What Braith, *what* do you want!?"

Jack's gaze rested on Aria. "He can protect himself, but if one of us, just *one* gets by him..."

"You don't have to worry about my family Braith, they won't hurt me," Aria assured him. "And you don't have to fear yours."

"Don't I?"

She shook her head, standing on tiptoe she pulled him down to her to make sure that he could hear her, but no one else could. "If they were going to harm you they would have done so by now. They may have kept things from you, but none of them meant for you to be hurt, in fact they've been trying to protect you for awhile. *Any*one of them could have tried to kill you in that palace."

"I'm not risking your life," he muttered.

"You won't be," she promised. "Just let her untie Ashby, Braith. I couldn't stand to see you like that either. They haven't earned your trust, not yet, but you haven't earned theirs either. This is a good way to start."

His jaw clenched, a muscle jumped in his cheek. For a brief moment his arms tensed around her, and then his grip relaxed. "Untie him," he ordered briskly. "But I will kill you both if you come anywhere near her."

Melinda stared at Aria for a long moment, her eyes filled with surprise and gratitude as she gave a small nod of appreciation. Then she turned to Ashby and her fingers flew deftly over the knots. Aria refused to look at her family; she could feel their horrified gazes she didn't have to see them. Ashby's hands came forward; he rubbed his wrists together as Melinda untied his ankles.

As the last of the ropes fell away, they embraced tightly, clinging to one another. Aria's heart went out to them, her hands clenched on Braith. She needed him so much, needed his embrace and touch and security. She yearned to run from here with him, and her family, but she had a feeling that wasn't going to happen. There was something changing

inside of Braith, something evolving and growing within him that frightened her.

She'd been well aware of the fact that he'd had no solid plan when
they'd fled those caves. He had a plan now, or at least he had some idea
of what he meant to do. The only problem was that his plan was going to
terrify her, and he was going to try and leave her out, of that much she
was certain.

"Aria?"

She turned toward her family, struggling to keep her tears at bay. Her
father was watching them fixedly, his head turned to the side as he
inspected her. He was normally clean shaven, but he had a couple days
worth of growth shadowing his strong jaw. His hair was dark auburn like
hers, and William's, but recently it had started to become streaked with
strands of white that also shadowed his beard. His eyes were a bright,
piercing green that had never failed to pin her to the spot and make her
squirm. Time had etched lines around his eyes and mouth, but he was
still a handsome man. Especially when he smiled, which wasn't very
often, and certainly wasn't now.

She longed to go to him, to all of them, but Braith's tension was too
high. "I'm ok dad, really."

She offered him a tremulous smile that did nothing to alleviate the
tension humming through him. Hatred simmered in his gaze as he
focused on Braith, but there was also confusion and disbelief. "This is
*the* prince?" he inquired scathingly.

Aria rested her hand on Braith's chest, trying to relieve the hostility
she felt rapidly building in him. She knew it wasn't going to be easy, but
her family would have to learn to trust him, as they had learned to trust
Jack. And Braith was going to have to learn to trust someone
besides *her*.

"One of them," Braith replied crisply. "The youngest one is standing
in front of you."

Her father's eyes darted to Jack, but he didn't acknowledge Braith's
words. "*You're* the one that claimed my daughter as a blood slave; *you're*
the one that took her this time also."

"Yes."

Fury flashed across her father's face. William and Daniel's eyes widened, but they didn't radiate the hatred her father did. "You held her, you tortured her..."

"I have told you many times that I was not tortured in there!" Aria interrupted sharply.

"I saw the bite mark!" her father snapped.

Aria blinked in surprise. Her hands tightened on Braith's arms, not to comfort him this time, but because she required his strength. "Everything I gave, I gave willingly," she said firmly, truthfully.

"Bullshit!"

It was not her father that exploded with those two words, but Max. Aria hadn't realized he was just outside the doorway, behind her father, Daniel, and William. He shoved his way forward now, pushing roughly past them as he shouldered his way into the room. Aria had never seen him look so crazed, and so completely out of control. His blue eyes were bulging and wild in his head, his hair stood up in disarray. Braith stiffened, pushing her back as Max charged at them.

Jack leapt forward, snagging hold of Max's arm as Braith released a snarl that caused even her heart to jump. Max swung on Jack, catching him sharply beneath his chin and knocking him back a small step. Jack was far stronger than Max, but he hadn't expected the punch and he was knocked off balance by it. Not only had he not expected the first punch, but he sure hadn't expected the one two combination that Max laid on him next.

Daniel and William were lunging at Max, but he had already shaken off Jack and was charging back at them. "You're *lying*!" he accused, his shoulders stiff as he barreled toward them. "He's twisted you! You're lying!"

Daniel, William, and Jack continued after him, but they were never going to stop him in time. Neither was Ashby as he pulled Melinda out of the way before lunging forward to make a failed grab at Max. Braith released her, pushing her behind him as he used his body to block her from Max's attack. Terror hammered through Aria, she could *not* allow this to happen. Max was out of his mind; he had been tortured and used as a blood slave, he had been abused in ways that she could never begin to imagine. Max didn't understand her love for Braith because he was convinced that Braith had done the same things to her.

"Wait! Stop!" she yelled.

Braith attempted to push her farther back but she ducked, dodging his arm as he tried to snag hold of her. She thrust herself forward, throwing herself in between Max and Braith. Unfortunately she hadn't seen what it was that Max wielded in his hand until it was too late. His arm was already flung forward, the metal blade whipped through the air even as she rose to her full height.

Braith's hand shot out in front of her. The blade slammed into his palm, driving through flesh and bone before bursting out the other side. Aria stared at it in horror. It was only a mere inch from the center of her forehead, exactly where Braith's heart was behind her. Though the metal blade wouldn't have killed Braith, it would have wounded him and knocked him back enough for Max to get to him, for Max to try and use the wooden stake he now wielded.

Aria's heart lumbered in her chest. Her eyes crossed as she stared at the awful blade before her, the one that would have killed her; the one that was still embedded in Braith's hand. It had to hurt like a bitch, but he showed no sign of that as he reached around her, grabbed hold of the blade and pulled it out. The scrape of metal on bone was loud in the room that had become deathly silent.

Blood trailed down Braith's hand, plopping loudly onto the wooden floor. Aria swallowed heavily, terrified of what was to come, terrified of what Braith's reaction would be. She could feel the deadly tension that vibrated through him. He was so infuriated that she didn't think she'd be able to stop him from killing Max. No one moved, no one even breathed.

Even Max, horrified by the fact that he had nearly killed her, seemed to have regained some control over himself. Braith, not surprisingly, was the first to react. He fisted his hand, twisting it before him. Aria was horrified by the blood that spilled freely from the large gash. She grabbed for him, but he seized hold of her hand, his touch surprisingly gentle for the pain he had to be suffering.

"Braith."

Aria could hear the nervous tension in Jack's voice. She understood it completely, though she couldn't see Braith's face, she could feel the murderous intent thrumming through him. Max took a small step back; Aria knew that what he was seeing had to be terrifying. Though he was large, temperamental, and powerful, Braith had always been relatively mellow and kind with her. That was who he was with *her*, but with others, and *to* others, he could be cruel, brutal, and lethal.

It was the lethal part that she was most frightened of now.

Aria turned, she had to see him, had to know what he was thinking. His eyes were a violent shade of red that caused Aria's knees to tremble as he focused on Max. His fangs had extended, but they didn't drop over his bottom lip. Instead, they were clamped behind his full mouth as a muscle jumped in his cheek.

He was terrifying, and deadly. "Braith, please," she whispered tremulously. His eyes flickered to her, but there was no easing of his features. "He didn't know what he was doing."

"He could have killed you," Braith grated.

"I wasn't going for her," Max retorted.

"Max, shut up!" Jack commanded.

"Well I wasn't."

Jack lunged forward; he seized hold of Max's arm and ripped him back. "You are an *idiot*."

"Let go of me!" Max snapped. "I'm going to kill him!"

Jack was struggling to get Max under control as a low growl rumbled up Braith's chest. Aria's head was spinning, the confusion in the room was mind numbing. Her father was grasping for Max, bitterness was etched into the lines of his face. "That's enough Maxwell!" her father commanded sharply.

But even her father, a man that had helped to raise Max, a man that Max highly respected and listened to, could not pierce the fury that enshrouded him. He continued to struggle, his face florid as a vein throbbed in his forehead. "He's corrupted her! He's made her a traitor, a disgrace to her own people, and he needs to die for his perversity!"

Aria recoiled from his words, feeling as if she'd been slapped, feeling as if *she* was the one that had been stabbed. For the first time she realized that Max would never forgive her for this. She had lost him forever. "You bitch!"

Aria gasped, but it was not Max's words that caused her reaction, but the sudden explosion of motion from behind her. She barely saw Braith, and she most certainly didn't hear him, as he sped across the room. Jack didn't have time to react, her father had one hand on Max's arm, but he wasn't strong enough to stop Braith from ripping Max back. Jack lunged gracefully forward, but it was too late. Braith was already spinning Max away from the others. He slammed Max against the wall with enough force that the entire room shook, and the wall splintered.

Melinda's hand flew to her mouth. Ashby swept past her as Braith pulled Max back before slamming him into the wall again. Ashby and Jack grasped hold of Braith's shoulders, but Aria knew they were nothing more than annoying gnats against him. "I don't care what was done to you!" Braith roared his face twisted in a mask of brutality the likes of which Aria had never seen before. "You hurt her, you talk to her, you so much as *look* at her again and you'll be dead before you even know what happened. Do you understand me you little shit!?"

His hand constricted on Max's throat, he lifted him off the ground and smashed him against the wall again. Aria was scared the building was going to collapse as it rocked on the stilt foundations. Max's eyes bulged, his fingers clawed at Braith's hand as his feet began to kick against the wall. "Braith!" Jack yelled, pulling uselessly at Braith's arm. "Let go! Damn it Braith, let *go*!"

Aria's bewildered stupor vanished. If she didn't do something, Braith was going to kill Max now. "Arianna!" Melinda cried as Aria ran toward Braith.

"Stop! Don't Braith! Please let him go!" She shoved her way past Ashby. Grabbing hold of Braith's arm, the one pinning Max to the wall, she gave a hard tug on it. It was like trying to bend iron; he barely noticed that she was there. Bracing her legs on the wall, she yanked on his arm. "He's my friend!" she cried in frustration. "Stop it, you're hurting him!"

Braith released Max so suddenly that Aria accidently shoved herself off the wall. She flew backward, losing her grasp on his arm as she tumbled back. Braith spun suddenly, his arms swooping around her, catching her before she could hit the floor. Max dropped like a weight, hitting the ground with a loud thump.

Aria gazed up at Braith in stunned disbelief. He had been so quick, so fast in catching her, and so gentle as he cradled her with a tenderness that robbed her of her breath. The red faded from his eyes, his fangs retreated as he looked lovingly upon her. He ignored the rest of them as he turned away, and strode with her across the room. The vampire girl was watching them in surprise, but there was a keen interest in her gaze that somewhat unnerved her.

Aria peeped around Braith's massive shoulder. Jack and Ashby were helping Max to his feet, he was rubbing his throat; the imprint of Braith's hand was clearly visible upon it. "I would stay quiet if you want to live!" Jack hissed at him when Max opened his mouth to say something more. "She won't be able to stop him again."

Aria ducked back away, she looked up at Braith. She had never been frightened of him, she had even slapped him once, but she was truly terrified for anyone that he felt was a threat to her. For the first time she realized the true depth of his desire to protect her. He had let Max go this time, but he would *not* do it again. Melinda studied them, her gaze disbelieving as she turned toward Braith, and then Ashby.

Aria saw the silent communication that passed between them, the intensity of their stares, and their concern. "Put me down Braith," she urged.

He slipped her easily from his arms, balancing her upon her feet. "Are you ok?" he inquired anxiously as he pushed her hair back away from her face to study her.

"I'm fine, I'm fine," she assured him hastily.

She grasped hold of his wounded hand, pulling it before her. He kept it fisted, but at her persistent prodding he reluctantly unfolded it. She gaped at him in astonishment, her mouth dropping as she rapidly fumbled with his hand. Blood still marred his skin, but there was nothing there. Not anymore. She stared in awe, unable to believe that what she was seeing was real. It was there, she knew a cut had been *there* but there wasn't even one scratch upon his flesh anymore. His hand curled around hers, he pulled her close for a brisk, firm kiss on her forehead.

"It's ok Arianna, I hardly felt a thing."

She gazed up at him, her mouth parted, astounded by the rate in which the wound had vanished. She knew that vampires were able to heal rapidly, but this was something not only stunning, and amazing, but also a little unnerving. She couldn't stop the shiver of trepidation that ran down her spine. "Braith?"

He kissed her again; his fingers lingered on the nape of her neck. "I'm good."

She squeezed his hand, wishing that they could go somewhere, wishing that they could be alone for just a few moments to recoup. Unfortunately, that was not possible right now. He turned away from her, and though he didn't try and block her from everyone again, he kept his hand on the wall by her head, and his other hand on her waist. She was well aware of the fact that he had kept himself in a better position to stop her if she tried to jump forward again.

She chafed against the invisible restraints he had placed on her and his protective urges but it would only irritate him more if she fought with him. Braith had to think that he was in control right now, even if he wasn't. Max was still in the grip of Ashby and Jack, but he wasn't trying to fight them anymore. He was simply staring at her and Braith as if they had just sprouted two heads, jumped on a table, and started dancing a jig while singing at the top of their lungs. Aria understood his reaction, if it had been anyone else from their camp, she would have felt the same way. But it wasn't anyone else, it was *her*, and she knew that what she felt for Braith was real, it was genuine, and it was so good and pure that it made them both stronger and better.

"It appears that we have a lot to discuss."

Aria looked across the room, trying to keep up the appearance of strength and courage, but her father was staring at her in a way that made her feel like a child all over again. She wanted to go to him, she wanted to hug him, she wanted to be his little girl for just one more minute, but she knew she could never be his little girl again. She wanted to apologize, wanted to tell her father that she had never wanted any of this, but she couldn't. It was true that the last thing she had expected was to fall in love with a vampire, but she wouldn't change any of it.

"Yes," she agreed.

# CHAPTER SEVENTEEN

"Our mother's family was nearly as powerful as our father's. They were married over a thousand years ago when the world was a different place, just as it was different a hundred years ago, before the war started. At the time of their marriage, superstition ruled, witches were burned, and our kind was relegated to the shadows. Our father always chafed against that, but he knew that to try and come out during those times would only result in death. So he waited. He bided his time, and he married our mother so that he would have more power, and more allies, for when the war broke out.

"And yes, I think that he was making plans to start it even back then," Jack said swiftly, cutting off Braith's question before he could ask it. "I think he planned it for even longer than that. He stayed with our mother, continued to have children with her. He had to keep up the pretense that he cared for her a little more than the rest of the nobles cared for their spouses, had to treat her well if he was going to keep her family as an ally.

"There was no king at this time, but a conglomerate of nobles that ran the underworld, dealt out the rules, and meted out punishments rapidly, and with imaginative, sickening flare. The nobles had grouped together to wrest control, and murder, the previous king. Before then the underworld had been nothing but a series of civil wars that had started to decimate the more powerful families as each king was brought down. Upon ousting the last king, it was decided that they would rule as a group in order to keep the inner slaughter somewhat under control.

"Our father had to find a way to wrest control from them if he was going to become the single, most powerful figure again."

"Shit!" Braith hissed.

Aria was staring wide eyed at Jack as he spoke. Though Braith seemed to have figured out where this was going, she still wasn't quite sure. Her hand shook in Braith's as he enfolded both of his around hers. She could feel an awful trembling working its way through her, but she couldn't stop it. "If you remember father was never cruel to mother, at least not publicly, and I have no idea what went on behind closed doors. So when he *did* turn on her, when he did accuse her of unfaithfulness and treachery no one questioned it, *everyone* believed him."

Aria was beginning to shake; she could feel it all the way down to the tips of her toes. She knew little of what the world had been like before the war. She'd heard stories of a world where humans ruled, there were libraries and schools, and homes and buildings that touched the sky. She had thought that most of it was a myth, stories filtered through the generations to entertain children, and to give people something to fight for. But listening to Jack, she had a feeling that there was so much more that she didn't know, and that she would never see.

No human seemed to know what had triggered the war that left the human population decimated, starving, and just barely clinging to survival, but she was beginning to realize that it was something that she had never even begun to fathom.

"For hundreds of years he bided his time, until he felt that the situation was becoming one that he could control, manipulate, and use to his advantage."

"And then he exiled her," Braith stated.

"Yes."

"And then he had her killed in order to fire the spark that started the war."

"Her family demanded revenge; they blamed the humans who had been set up to take the fall for her murder. Father was able to take control of the situation, manipulating everyone to his way. He may have exiled her, but she was still his wife, and it was still his *daughter* that had been so ruthlessly slaughtered."

Aria gasped in astonishment as she focused on Melinda. The beautiful woman was standing proudly, her chin raised defiantly. She showed no sign that the fact her father had expected her to be killed in the raid upset her. However, no matter how much time had passed, no matter how much she despised the father that had helped create her, Aria knew that it still had to hurt her. The small flicker in her dove colored eyes revealed this.

"They allowed him to seize the power and rule that father had always coveted," Braith said.

"And once he took it there was no stopping him," Melinda murmured.

Aria shuddered, the night was warm, but she was suddenly freezing cold. Her bones were numb; she was barely able to stand anymore. She could feel the shock radiating from Braith at the depths of his father's perfidy. "How long have you known this?" he inquired.

Jack shifted; he looked uncomfortable by the amount of hostility radiating from Braith. "About sixty years. It took me awhile to gather all the pieces of the story and to actually believe it. I hate the man, there's never been any love lost between us, but even *I* had a tough time believing that he would have our mother killed for his own advancement."

Braith closed his eyes for a moment. Aria ached for him, she ached to comfort him, but this was not the time, and it was not the place. Later, when they were alone, she would try and take some of his suffering from him, but she wasn't certain that even she could help ease this treachery and loss.

"Your family is even more screwed up than ours," William muttered.

Jack cocked an eyebrow at him; a sad smile curved his mouth. "And you haven't had the pleasure of meeting Caleb, or Natasha, yet."

William nodded slowly; his gaze drifted to Aria. "What did you get yourself into now sis?"

Aria managed a weak smile; William was trying to sound casual, but even his normal jovial tone fell short in this horrendous mess. She itched to go to William, to hug him and the rest of her family. However Braith wasn't ready to let her go just yet. "Braith." She rubbed his arm, looking to comfort him, looking to get him to relax a little. It didn't seem to be working.

"You know everything now Braith, you know what was done, and you know what we believe. The question now is; what are you going to do?" Jack asked pointedly.

Braith's beautiful eyes were aglow in the dim room. The blue in them was bright, sharp in contrast to the unrelenting gray. There was something in his gaze, something so vulnerable and yet so strong that she felt her insides melt. His eyes caressed her face, stroking lovingly over her, but the steel rod of determination within his eyes left her cold with dread. "Braith," she breathed.

"I'm going to keep you safe."

She managed a small nod. "I know you will. I have absolute faith in that."

"No matter what, Arianna, I am going to keep you safe."

She gulped; her heart was fluttering rapidly. "It's a brutal war to wage," she whispered, a war that he had not experienced in a hundred years; a war that she had only lived through the horrendous consequences of.

"It is. The results of the last war have to be set right though."

"They will follow you Braith," Jack encouraged.

Aria shot him a dark, withering look. She knew what Braith had in mind, knew that she couldn't stop him, but Jack didn't have to make him feel as if he *had* to do it, because he didn't. She would stand by him no matter what he decided. Even if he decided he chose to flee from here and never look back. That may not be her choice, but she would support it because she supported *him*. It wouldn't be her that would be going against her own family; she wouldn't force him into that position.

"Will they Jack?" Braith inquired dryly.

Jack swallowed heavily as Braith leveled him with a virulent stare. "Yes. I think you may be as strong as father now." Jack focused upon her. Braith stiffened and stepped in front of her. "Maybe even stronger. Many will look to you for leadership, especially the vampires on the outskirts, especially the ones starving under father's regime."

"And the people will follow the human," Braith said coldly. Aria shivered at his harsh, brutal tone. "Isn't that right Jack?"

"They will."

"Why do I feel as if I have been manipulated into this?" he grated.

"As if anyone could have expected you to fall in love with your blood slave," Melinda retorted.

"I am *not* a blood slave!" Aria snapped.

"Maybe not anymore, but you were. It's how all of this started after all."

Aria glared at her. "*No* one saw that coming," Jack agreed, trying to placate everyone with his docile tone.

"I don't think they'll follow a vampire who fell for their blood slave." Braith squeezed Aria's hand reassuringly when he said the words blood slave. "In fact, I imagine most of them will be disgusted by it."

"That is one thing we will have to keep secret," Jack agreed. Anger and hurt bloomed through Aria's chest but she tilted her chin defiantly. She would have to stay strong, she would have to accept that fact if they were going to succeed, and if they were ever going to have any chance at happiness they would *have* to succeed. "For now it will have to look as if you have formed an alliance with the humans, and as if you are going to bring the peace and security to the vampire race that father promised, but was unable to provide. The humans will follow if they are assured safety and security, which we will give them. When this is all over..."

"When this is all over, the two of us will be going somewhere safe. When this is all over, we *will* be left alone," Braith interrupted sharply.

Jack was hesitant; Aria could barely look at her family. They were staring at her with a mixture of confusion and defeat that made her ache for them. "They'll follow *you* Braith," Melinda whispered.

He kept Aria behind him still, unwilling to expose her to anything he might consider a threat. "And they'll follow Jack after, and the humans will continue to follow one of them." Braith waved a hand lazily at her father and brothers.

"Yes, fine. We can work it all out later," Jack assured him quickly. Ashby looked about to protest, but Melinda rested a hand on his arm and shook her head subtly. Aria understood that look, understood what it meant. Braith might want to believe that they would be free *if* they somehow managed to succeed, but they all understood what Braith was trying desperately to deny. The two of them would never be free. "First things first though."

"Father has to come out of power, and Caleb has to be neutralized," Braith stated.

Aria squeezed his arm; he glanced down at her, the hard lines of his face smoothing out as he smiled at her. She smiled back before slipping past him toward her family. She was timid; frightened of the reaction she would get from them. It was William that stepped forward first to hug her against him. She sighed contentedly, embracing her twin as Daniel and her father came forward.

Relief and love filled her. It was a long, savage road they all had ahead of them, but they could do this together. With the love of her family, with the love of Braith, she could get through anything.

Her gaze drifted back to Braith. She couldn't resist him. Releasing her family, she rejoined him, wrapping her arms around his waist as she buried her head in his chest. The coming war was inevitable; she would be giving up everything to help wage it, including Braith. She was acutely aware of the fact that when all of this was over, there would be little left for them. It was *him* that had to rule, they all saw that already, even if he didn't. And as a human, she would have no place by his side.

But she couldn't think about that now, there was a war to fight first.

### The End.

**Book 3 in this series, Refugee, is now available!**
**Refugee on Amazon:** http://bit.ly/RfgAmz

Stay in touch on updates and new releases from the author by joining the mailing list!
**Mailing list for Erica Stevens & Brenda K. Davies Updates:**
http://bit.ly/ESBKDNews

# FIND THE AUTHOR

Erica Stevens/Brenda K. Davies Mailing List:
http://bit.ly/ESBKDNews

Facebook page: http://bit.ly/ESFBpage
Facebook friend: http://bit.ly/EASFrd

Erica Stevens/Brenda K. Davies Book Club:
http://bit.ly/ESBDbc

Instagram: http://bit.ly/ErStInsta
Twitter: http://bit.ly/ErStTw
Website: http://bit.ly/ESWbst
Blog: http://bit.ly/ErStBl

# ABOUT THE AUTHOR

Erica Stevens is the author of the Captive Series, Kindred Series, Fire & Ice Series, Ravening Series, and the Survivor Chronicles. She enjoys writing young adult, new adult, romance, horror, and science fiction. She also writes adult paranormal romance and historical romance under the pen name, Brenda K. Davies. When not out with friends and family, she is at home with her husband, dog, and horse.

27584180R00103

Printed in Great Britain
by Amazon